SURROUNDED BY THE
BLUE

A Novel of Ocean Adventure and Survival
by
VICTOR ZUGG

SURROUNDED BY THE BLUE

VictorZuggAuthor@gmail.com

ACKNOWLEDGEMENTS

Many thanks to Brandi Doane McCann for the cover design and Tamra Crow for the professional editing. They both made the book infinitely better.

Brandi: **www.ebook-coverdesigns.com**
Tamra: **tcrowedits@yahoo.com**

CHAPTER 1

The heavy airliner floated smoothly, almost magically, toward the wet tarmac racing up to meet the extended landing gears. Smoke and steam bellowed as rubber touched concrete. Reverse thrusters roared and the large mass slowed until finally it turned onto a taxiway and rolled through the early afternoon drizzle toward the terminal.

The plane came to a complete stop with a slight curtsy. The jetway extended to meet the fuselage, and passengers disembarked.

Michelle Stewart, Mickey to her friends, was one of those passengers. Dressed in business attire tailored around her slender five-foot six-inch frame, she wheeled a soft-sided carry-on through the throngs of people, all headed in the same direction down the corridor. She walked with purpose; a bounce in every step.

She exited the glass doors ahead of the crowd and went straight for a taxi idling at the curb. The driver standing next to the open door smiled as Mickey made eye contact. She slid into the rear seat and lowered her bag to the floor.

The driver slammed the door, hoofed it around to his side, and plopped behind the wheel. He swiped at the meter on the dash, did likewise to the gearshift, and then eased into a steady stream of traffic. "Where to?" he asked, with only a slight Caribbean accent.

"Fifty-ninth and eighth, please," she said, without looking up. She pulled a leather-bound note pad from a zippered compartment, and began reading, flipping pages occasionally.

The taxi pulled to a stop in front of a tall, older granite building, adorned with reliefs. The building stood in stark contrast to the newer glass and steel to each side.

Mickey pulled some bills from a wallet and handed them to the driver.

The driver nodded, "Thanks."

"Thank you," Mickey said, as she opened the taxi door, wiggled out, and pulled her bag along behind her. She pushed through the glass doors, entered an elevator in the lobby, and pushed the button for the twenty-first floor.

The elevator door opened and Mickey stepped into a rich, marble and mahogany foyer furnished with equally rich chairs, sofas, and tables. Double glass doors, etched with *Jackson Advertising*, opened into a second foyer. A young attractive blond wearing a headset spoke into the microphone as Mickey approached the counter and continued to a side door.

The girl smiled and waved at Mickey, while continuing to speak into the microphone.

As Mickey reached for the handle, the door buzzed and then clicked. Mickey pulled the door open, waved back at the girl behind the counter, and stepped into a carpeted corridor lined with offices. Men and women occupied desks in front of most of the offices. All were busy typing on computers or talking on the phone. Several of the people looked up and smiled as Mickey passed. She smiled back, or nodded or both, to each person as they continued their work.

About midway down the corridor Mickey approached a middle-aged woman sitting behind a desk. The name plate on the desk read *Janet Summers*. Her eyes fixated on papers to one side of her computer as her fingers danced around the keyboard in a blur. She paused and looked up as Mickey stopped in front of the desk. "Mickey, you're back early. How did it go?"

"Not sure, they're thinking about it," Mickey said. "But it looks promising."

"I'm sure they will buy. It's a great campaign."

"Do you know if Jack's in his office?" Mickey asked.

"I saw him head out about an hour ago, probably for the day," Janet replied.

Mickey glanced at her wrist watch. "It's only three o'clock; must have had a meeting."

Janet smiled slightly, nodded, and then continued with her work as Mickey proceeded into her office.

Mickey took a seat in her chair and a moment to relax. She leaned back and stared at the ceiling. She thought about the trip. There was a very good chance she had brought in what could be a very large account that would continue for years. The company's executive staff seemed genuinely impressed with her presentation and the proposal. She had worked on it for weeks, day and night. Jack and the ad panel thought it was imaginative, brilliant even, and would do what all ads were intended to do: increase revenue.

Mickey closed her eyes for a few moments, and then sat forward in her chair. She faced her computer, pushed the on button, and saw the screen almost immediately come to life. She never ceased to be amazed at the speed of the solid-state drive. She waited a few moments and then started punching keys. She wanted mostly to see if the proposal team had followed up while she was on the plane. Seeing nothing from them, or anything else that couldn't wait until the next day, she pushed the power button to turn off the machine. Many of her coworkers just left their machines on while they were out of the office, but she was wary of the potential for viruses and such, and preferred her machine to be off when she wasn't around. The screen blinked to black.

She stood up, grabbed her carry-on bag, and walked to the outer office. "I'm heading out a little early," she said to Janet. "See you in the morning."

"Have a nice evening," Janet replied, and then turned back to her computer.

***

Mickey, behind the wheel of a red BMW, pulled into a circular drive and stopped in front of a large glass and stone home, complete with a manicured lawn and fountain. She noticed the Mercedes sport coupe already parked in the drive. The vanity plate on the Mercedes read, "*JACKS ADS*."

She used her key to open the front door. Pulling her suitcase, she entered the large foyer. She left the suitcase at the door and immediately headed up the carpeted stairs leading to the bedrooms on the second floor.

At the top of the stairs she turned toward the master bedroom. That's when she heard the sounds, from behind the slightly opened door. A man and a woman.

Mickey quietly approached, peered through the crack, and then pushed the door, slowly widening the opening until the door was completely open.

She stared at Paul (Jack) Jackson, nude, on top of a young blond, also nude. Her feet were wide apart, pointed at the ceiling, as Jack's hips pounded up and down between her thighs. Her butt pressed into the mattress with each of Jack's downward thrusts. The muscles in his legs, back, and outstretched arms flexed with every motion. Her breasts bounced side to side. Sweat pooled on her flat stomach. Her eyes were closed.

Suddenly he stopped, arched his back, and let out a long, slow moan.

The woman immediately wrapped her legs around his butt, flung her arms around his neck, and pulled his upper body down. Sweat dripped from their skin. Then, she too arched her back and pressed her head into the pillow while she sucked air between her clenched teeth. She held that position, and her breath, for several seconds until she slowly began to relax and exhale.

Jack rolled to her side, toward Mickey, until he was flat on his back, head turned toward the woman. The woman took a few deep breaths, blinked her eyes open, and turned her head toward Jack. Her eyes went wide.

Jack apparently realized the change in her expression. He twisted his head and looked over his shoulder.

Mickey locked eyes with Jack for a moment and then wiped the tears that ran down her cheeks.

Jack jumped to his feet and started toward Mickey.

Mickey turned and stepped back into the hall.

"Mickey," Jack said, in a raised, excited voice. "Wait."

Mickey hurried down the stairs with Jack, still nude, close behind.

"Mickey, it meant nothing," Jack said.

"It meant something to me," Mickey said, as she reached the bottom of the stairs, grabbed her suitcase, and wheeled it out the front door. She threw the suitcase in the backseat of her car, slammed the door, opened the driver's door, and got in. She glanced toward the house.

Jack stood in the open doorway, staring at Mickey.

Mickey inserted the key and turned; the engine purred to life. She rolled down the driver's window. "You're an asshole," she yelled.

Jack opened his mouth to say something, but then closed it without saying anything as the car window rolled closed.

Mickey wiped more tears, shifted the gear, and continued around the circular drive back to the road.

***

Weeping, Mickey slouched behind the wheel of her car, parked in an underground garage. Her cell phone rang. She pulled the phone from her purse and checked the caller ID. *Jack*. She replaced the phone without answering. The phone rang again and then stopped. Mickey wiped away her tears with a tissue, composed herself, and started the car.

Mickey pulled into Jack's driveway for the second time that day. She stopped the car half way to the house and contemplated what she should do. Go in, or keep driving? She put the gear in drive, but kept her foot on the brake, and then cupped her face with both hands. She had no place to go. No real friends. No family in the area.

She remembered when she first met Jack. She was a recent graduate with a marketing degree from the mid-west, determined to make it in the big city. She had applied to numerous agencies, was on the verge of giving up, when she got the offer from Jack. That was over five years ago. Even though Jack had taken a special interest in her, she worked hard, learned the business, and moved up, all while trying to keep her relationship with Jack on a professional level. She kept that up for just over three years, but he finally wore her down with the flowers, dinners, and more. She finally gave up her tiny flat and moved in just over a year ago. Despite his flirtations and a minor dalliance, she loved him, and thought he loved her. Apparently, she thought wrong.

Mickey entered the foyer and immediately heard the clang of dishes from the kitchen. She entered the kitchen and saw Jack with a beer in one hand and a plate with a sandwich in the other. Mickey stopped in the doorway.

Jack looked up, saw Mickey, and immediately started toward her as he put the beer and plate on the table. "Mickey Moo, I'm sorry, it will never happen again. I love you." He put his arms around her.

Mickey lightly pushed him back and then stared into his eyes. "Yeah, I know."

She turned, walked back toward the foyer, and then up the stairs. At the open door to the master bedroom she stopped and stared at the made up bed for several seconds. She then marched over and ripped the comforter, sheets, and mattress pad off of the bed, tossed the linens in a corner, and then stomped to the corner of the room farthest from the bed. She slid her butt down the wall to the floor and cried.

***

Mickey stood gazing out her office window at the New York skyline. The sky was overcast, but no rain. She glanced down at the street and watched the vehicles and people buzzing about. She then looked back at her desk, at the large vase containing two-dozen red roses. She moved to her chair, took a seat, and spun around to face her desk. She looked at the roses again and then wiped tears from her cheeks.

She picked up her phone handset and punched a series of numbers. The phone rang at the other end and then a woman answered.

"It's me," Mickey said, "how are you doing?"

"Your favorite sister is doing just fine, but you don't sound particularly happy."

Mickey sniffled. "Susan, you're not only my favorite sister, you're my only sister, in fact, you're my only family."

"He cheated on you again, didn't he?" Susan asked.

"Uh-huh," Mickey said, still sniffling.

"Mickey, why do you put up with him? You're not married to the asshole. You're not married, right?"

"No, I'm not married, but I do love him."

"Maybe so," Susan said. "But he obviously doesn't love you, at least not in the way you deserve to be loved."

"Why do I pick the wrong men?"

There was a pause on Susan's end of the line.

"What am I doing wrong?"

"Look, why don't you just get away for a while?" Susan said. "You know Thomas and I are heading out on the boat. Why don't you come along?"

Mickey paused, looked to the ceiling, and then let out a long exhale. "I don't know, I have so much work. Let me think about it."

"Okay, but we leave in three days. I'd love for you to join us. Thomas would love it, too."

There was a knock on Mickey's door and then the door cracked open. Jack stuck his head in and smiled.

"I have a visitor," Mickey said into the phone. "I'll call you back."

"Soon," Susan said.

"Soon," Mickey said. "I love you." She hung up the phone.

She spun around in her chair and looked out the window at the darkening clouds.

Jack walked around the desk and knelt down by Mickey's chair. He stared at Mickey's face. "I'm really sorry, forgive me?" After a few beats with no response from Mickey, he said, "It will never happen again, I promise. I really do love you. Only you."

Mickey continued to look out the window, without making eye contact.

"Okay, I'll leave you alone for a while," Jack said. "Let's go out to a nice restaurant tonight?"

Mickey said nothing. She continued to stare out the window.

"It's on me," Jack said with a smile.

Mickey did not respond.

Jack stood and walked to the door. "I'll check on you later."

Mickey gazed at her hands clasped in her lap. "I may visit Susan for awhile."

Jack paused at the door. "I was hoping we could spend more time together and work this out. Plus, you need to follow up on the Bradley campaign. There's a lot of work to be done. We can talk about it tonight at home." Jack stepped out and eased the door shut.

Mickey gazed out the window a few more seconds, and then turned back to her desk. She picked up the phone and punched some numbers.

Susan answered.

"It's me," Mickey said. "I've thought about it. I'll call you later with my arrival time."

"Mickey, that's wonderful," Susan said. "You'll have a great time. Maybe you'll even find adventure and true romance."

"Adventure, maybe," Mickey said. "Romance, I doubt it. Like you said, I just need to get away for awhile. I'll see you at the airport."

"We love you, Mickey," Susan said. "See you soon."

"I love you, too."

Mickey put the phone in the cradle and then punched her intercom button. "Janet, I need a ticket to LA for today. Put it on my personal credit card and leave the return open. Give me enough time to go home and pack a few things."

"It's about time you took some time for yourself," Janet said. "One ticket coming up. What about the Bradley campaign?"

"Jack will have to handle it," Mickey said. "Give him a hand with anything he needs. You know the campaign as well as I do."

"Like I said, one ticket coming up," Janet said. "Will you be going out on your sister's sailboat, the trip you told me about?

"Yeah, I'll leave you the name of the marina and a phone number. We'll be stopping in Hilo, on the big island. I can get off there or continue with them, south toward Samoa."

"I'll get that ticket before everything's booked," Janet said.

Mickey stood up, grabbed her purse, and marched out.

***

Mickey, sitting on the edge of the bed in the master bedroom, put the finishing touches on a notepad. She then leaned the pad against the nightstand lamp.

Jack, I think some time apart is best. I'm leaving today to stay with Susan for awhile. I'm not sure for how long. Don't worry. M

Mickey zipped her suitcase shut, took a few seconds to look around the room, and then walked out, dragging the case. She turned the lights off as she left the room.

CHAPTER 2

Mickey emerged from the terminal with a large group and immediately spotted Susan running toward her with arms open. Susan looked the same as she did the last time Mickey saw her, over two years earlier. At thirty-five she looked stunning with her pretty face, slender physique, and shoulder-length blond hair. Except for Susan being six years older, they looked a lot alike.

Susan wrapped her arms around Mickey and hugged her without saying a word. She then took a step back, gazed at Mickey's face a few moments, and then hugged her again. Susan finally released her and stepped back. "I'm so glad you're here. It's been too long."

"I know," Mickey said. "I've really missed you. And thanks for helping me through this."

"I'm just glad you're here. Thomas is driving circles, so we better get your suitcase."

Mickey pointed at her carry-on bag. "I travel light."

Susan smiled, spun around, and stepped closer to the curb as she peered down the lanes of oncoming traffic. After a few seconds she began waving for a shiny new Toyota SUV, which pulled to the curb next to her.

Thomas hopped out, ran around to the curbside, and gave Mickey a hug. "How was your flight?"

"Okay," Mickey said. "Just glad to be here."

"We're glad you could take some time off," Thomas said. "You'll love the boat."

Mickey nodded as Thomas picked up her bag and put it in the back seat. She then slid in beside it.

Susan and Thomas got in and Thomas checked his mirror before pulling into the stream of traffic. Mickey admired how Thomas kept himself in great shape. At forty, he was handsome, lean, and toned. His hair was dark, with a few more streaks of gray than the last time Mickey saw him. Susan and Thomas were the proverbial active couple, made easier since neither wanted kids.

"We're off to Newport," Susan said. "A good night's sleep, a bit of shopping tomorrow, and we'll be on the boat Saturday morning."

"You'll love the boat," Thomas said. "Just picked it up last month. Lots of room."

Susan glanced back at Mickey. "He's excited about the boat, and that you're here to witness the maiden voyage."

"I'm looking forward to some down time," Mickey said.

"Do you want to talk about it?" Susan asked.

"Maybe later," Mickey replied.

"Well, just some food for thought… he's a jerk."

Mickey nodded and then turned her head to gaze out the window.

***

Susan, dressed in shorts, tennis shoes, and a light top, hair pulled back in a ponytail, poured a cup of coffee as Mickey walked into the kitchen. Mickey, wearing capris, sandals, and a designer top, took a seat at the table.

"Want some?" Susan asked.

"Love some, still just black."

Susan poured another cup of coffee and delivered them to the table. She took a seat and covered Mickey's hand with her own. "Trust me; this is just what you need."

Mickey turned her hand, squeezed Susan's hand, and nodded. "I know. Where's Thomas?"

"A few last-minute things at the office."

"How's work?" Mickey asked.

"We're both busy, but that's the price of fame and glory."

The corners of Mickey's mouth turned up slightly, and then turned more somber. "I found Jack in bed again, my bed this time."

"Oh, Mickey, I'm so sorry." Susan took Mickey's hand again.

"I'm sure if Mom were still here she would be kicking my butt for putting up with him."

"She would," Susan said. "You'll get through this, and you can always count on me."

Mickey looked up from her coffee and gazed into Susan's eyes. "I know. I wouldn't know what to do without you."

"You're stronger than you think," Susan patted Mickey's hand. "We need to stock the boat, groceries and things. Adventure awaits."

Mickey took a deep breath and exhaled. "I'm ready, just point me in the right direction."

***

Susan and Mickey carried two bags of groceries each as they approached the docks. Mickey followed Susan, while examining the mass of boats. Some smaller boats bobbed gently in the water.

Mickey glanced toward the sky. "Do we have enough sunscreen?"

"We already have plenty on the boat," Susan said, as she continued along, passing boat after boat. Finally, she stopped next to a large sailboat and put her bags down on the dock. She stood back up and motioned toward the boat with both hands. "Ta dah!"

Mickey gazed at the boat, bow to stern, and then to the top of the mast. "Wow. What is it?

"Hallberg-Rassy 48 Mark II," Susan said. "She's pre-owned, but in excellent shape. Very sea worthy. We kept the name. Roundabout."

"It's so big," Mickey said.

Susan stepped over the guardrail and planted her feet on the deck. "Hand me the bags and then watch your step when you come aboard. It can be a little tricky at first."

Mickey handed Susan her two bags, and then the two bags from the dock. She then stepped aboard. "This isn't too bad," she said, with both feet on the teak deck.

"We're not moving," Susan said, as she turned toward the cockpit. "Let's put this stuff away and then I'll give you the grand tour."

Mickey pursed her lips, grabbed two bags, and followed.

Susan led Mickey into the cockpit, past the wheel, and down the ladder. She entered the saloon and placed her two bags on the mahogany table in the middle of the room. She immediately started emptying the bags and placing the items in various lockers.

Mickey sat her bags on the table and began removing various items. "Doesn't seem like very much food. How long is the trip to Hilo?"

"If the weather remains as it is, probably ten days or so, and then on to points south, another ten or fifteen days," Susan said. "You can stay with us for the entire round trip, or get off at Hilo or Samoa."

"Do we have enough food?"

"Not yet," Susan said. "We'll stop for more in the morning on our way to the dock. Actually, we only need enough for the first leg."

Susan finished stowing the various items while Mickey turned in a slow circle, admiring the interior.

"Mostly all mahogany," Susan said.

"It's beautiful."

Susan stepped back to the ladder and pointed at the galley. "This is the galley, complete with a double sink, three-burner gas stove, oven, and a fridge down below." Susan opened and closed the refrigerator. "And we have a microwave above the stove."

Mickey opened the microwave door and closed it.

"Directly across from the galley is the navigation station, or chart table." Susan then stepped toward the front of the boat. "Moving forward, we have sofas on both sides of the table. The table edge lifts up and we can add a couple of folding chairs, if needed."

Mickey ran her hand over the top of the wood table as she followed Susan into a narrow passageway.

Susan opened a door on the right. "Cabin with bunk beds. The top bunk folds up if not needed." She turned to the left and opened another door. "Bathroom, or head, as it's called on a boat. We have two. This one, and one in the aft cabin."

Mickey stepped into the head and looked around. "It even has a shower."

"A lot of the time we just bathed off the transom with seawater on our previous boats, to save fresh water, especially when the weather is warm."

"How much water does it hold?" Mickey asked.

"Two hundred and forty-one gallons, which is really not that much," Susan said. "We'll also have plenty of bottled water. And we have a water maker on board. It will make fresh water from sea water."

Mickey nodded as Susan opened a door at the end of the passageway. "This is the forward cabin. You can sleep here if you want, but the bunk beds have less up and down motion. By the way, to be safe, we need to get you some seasickness medicine. Even Thomas and I take it, sometimes."

Mickey stepped forward and peered into the cabin. "Looks like a lot of storage space."

"Lockers along both bulkheads."

Mickey nodded as she stepped back into the passageway.

"The main cabin is in the rear, or aft, section," Susan said, as she began walking in that direction. With Mickey following, Susan walked back through the saloon, past the galley and chart table, and down another narrow passageway. She stopped in the middle of the passageway and opened a locker on the port side bulkhead. "There's a little space here if anything needs to be hung."

Mickey nodded as Susan opened a door at the end of the passageway and stepped in.

"This is the aft main cabin where Thomas and I sleep," Susan said. "There's a double berth on the starboard, and a single on the port. If the weather gets too rough, you can sleep back here. This section rides a little easier in the waves." Susan pointed to a door at the head of the double bed. "The second bathroom is in there." Susan led Mickey out of the cabin, down the passageway, and into the saloon. "That's about it."

Mickey gazed around the room. "It's really beautiful, sis. Thank you for inviting me along."

"We're happy to have you," Susan said. "Someone to talk to in addition to Thomas will be a blessing." Susan motioned for Mickey to have a seat at the table. "Want something to drink?"

"Maybe just some water."

Susan pulled a jug of water from a shelf, poured two glasses, and then took a seat on the opposite sofa.

"Do you ever think about Mom and Dad?" Mickey asked.

"Mom, all the time," Susan said. "Dad, I try not to."

"I think of them both," Mickey said.

***

The seven-year-old girl with blond curls and a teddy bear tucked under her arm giggled as she tried to run past the man standing before her with open arms. As she tried to pass, the man grabbed her by the waist, swept her off her feet, and then spun around.

"I've got you, Mickey Moo," the man said, as he chortled.

Mickey giggled even more.

A woman, early thirties, wearing jeans and a button down top, entered the room at that moment and came to a stop a few feet from the man and Mickey. The woman put her hands on her hips with a smirk. "You two are going to break something."

The man put Mickey on the floor, knelt in front of her, gave her a hug, and then separated, still holding her shoulders. "Your mom is right." He then leaned in. "Meet you here after dinner for round two," he whispered.

Mickey smiled and then giggled.

The man stood, turned to the woman, and then leapt at her. "And now it's your turn," he said with a wry smile.

The woman laughed, turned, and dashed out of the room, followed by the man and Mickey.

***

Susan took a sip of water and then set the glass back on the table. "You were only ten when he left."

"Do you think Mom died because he left?"

"Maybe," Susan said. "He broke her heart. He broke your heart, too."

"What about you?"

"I was older, but it still hurt."

"I guess I've been trying to replace him," Mickey said.

"You think?" Susan said. "And they've all cheated on you, just like Dad cheated on Mom."

"And I hang around, just like Mom did."

"With two kids to care for, she just hoped he'd grow a brain and come home," Susan said. "He never did. The only person you can change is yourself."

"You sound like Doctor Phil."

"It's true," Susan said.

Mickey nodded.

Susan got to her feet and put both empty glasses in the sink. "We have more shopping to do."

"I could use something for the boat," Mickey said.

"Bikini and deck shoes are pretty much all you will need for the boat," Susan said. "Let's go see how much damage we can do."

***

Thomas sat at the dining table, set for dinner, perusing a chart when Susan and Mickey entered carrying bowls of food. They placed the bowls on the table, took a seat, and started spooning food onto their plates.

"We'll eat, you study the map."

"Chart," Thomas said.

Susan passed a bowl to Mickey. "Sorry. You study the chart."

Thomas folded the chart, put it aside, and began spooning food onto his plate.

"How far, and how long, is the cruise?" Mickey asked.

"Newport to Hilo—" Thomas took a bite and chewed.

"The fun is in the journey," Susan said.

"Twenty-two hundred miles to Hilo, another twenty-five hundred or so to Samoa," Thomas said, with his mouth still full. "Fifteen days, give or take, to Hilo. Six to eight weeks for the whole trip, Samoa and back."

"She's a fast boat," Susan said, as she glanced at Mickey. "You'll love the way she slips through the water."

Mickey pushed food around her plate with her fork. "That seems like a long time. And taking a bath in the middle of the ocean, what about sharks? What about water and power?"

"Plenty of water," Thomas said. "And the boat has a more than adequate battery pack, along with solar panels and wind and water turbines for charging. Plus, she has a separate generator when needed. We'll be fine."

"What about at night, does someone have to stay up all night?" Mickey asked.

Thomas finished chewing. "The autopilot does most of the work, night and day, unless I want to take the wheel. The boat has GPS, automatic identification, and radar. I'll get an alarm if we get too close to something. She has state-of-the-art equipment. No worries."

"Have you heard from Jack?" Susan asked.

"Turned my cell phone off."

"Are you going to call him before we leave in the morning?"

"Haven't decided. He knows I'm coming back. It may be his house, but my clothes and car are there. I took a taxi to the airport."

Thomas finished eating, retrieved the chart, and began perusing again.

Mickey and Susan finished eating, refilled their wine glasses, and sipped, while Mickey stacked the empty plates.

"Do you think I should call him?"

"I think you should leave him," Susan said. "He's a jerk. I mean, look at you. You could be a model. And you're the nicest person I know. But I'm not going to give advice. It's up to you."

"For the next five seconds, maybe, after that all bets are off," Thomas said sarcastically.

Susan glared at Thomas and then looked back at Mickey. "I'm your sister, and I'll always be here for you."

"I know, and I really appreciate that."

Susan touched Mickey's hand and then stood up. "Shall we clear the table?"

Susan and Mickey began ferrying the dirty dishes to the kitchen.

Thomas got up and started out of the room. "I'll be in the den, going over the charts."

"He can stare at those things for hours," Susan said to Mickey.

CHAPTER 3

Thomas stood in the cockpit, at the wheel, with the early morning sun on his face. Mickey was on the dock at the stern line; Susan at the bowline. Both wore light cotton shorts, a T-shirt, and deck shoes. The boat's Volvo engine purred at idle.

"Unhitch the lines and jump aboard," Thomas said in a raised voice.

Mickey and Susan unhitched the lines, hopped aboard, and immediately began coiling the ropes on the deck.

Thomas eased the throttle forward and turned the wheel as the boat inched away from the dock.

Mickey walked forward along the port deck and joined Susan at the bow. They both took a seat on the deck at the bow.

Thomas steered the boat through the various channels toward the open sea.

Mickey and Susan occasionally waved as they passed fellow yachters engaged in various activities on the boats tied to the docks. Soon the boat slipped past the docks and glided toward the horizon. Mickey and Susan joined Thomas in the cockpit and gazed at the Newport yacht harbor as it grew smaller in the distance.

Well offshore, Thomas turned the boat into the wind and killed the engine. He then adjusted some lines, checked their placement a second and third time, and then pushed a button. Mickey watched as the main sail unfurled. Thomas adjusted some more lines, double checked their placement, and then pushed another button. Mickey watched as the jib unfurled.

Thomas turned the wheel and let the sails catch the wind until he was back on a southwesterly heading. He then made minor adjustments to trim both sheets. Finally, he winked and smiled. "Nothing to it."

"I thought it would be much harder," Mickey said. She had to raise her voice above the wind.

"Not when you have electric equipment," Susan said.

"What happens if the electric doesn't work?" Mickey asked.

"The sails can be furled and unfurled with a hand crank, if necessary," Thomas said. "I'll show you how it works if you want."

"Yes," Mickey said. "I'd love to know more about the operation of the boat."

"We'll have plenty of time," Thomas said.

Mickey held onto the teak-covered coach roof and turned her face to the wind. Her short blond hair blew wild and free. She felt the rhythm of the boat as it sliced through the water. Occasionally, spray from the waves spritzed her face, a welcome reprieve from the sun.

Soon, Catalina Island was visible off the starboard bow, and then San Clemente Island off the port, as Thomas steered more westerly.

Thomas turned to face Mickey and Susan. "Looks like we're off and running."

"This is fantastic," Mickey said.

"Did you take the seasickness pills?" Susan asked.

"I did," Mickey said. "So far, so good."

"We'll see how you feel when we go below," Susan said.

Mickey dropped her chin slightly and raised an eyebrow.

"You'll be fine," Susan said. "I'm going below. Need to start getting organized."

"I'll set up the autopilot and be down in a bit," Thomas said.

"How does the autopilot work?" Mickey asked.

"It's a mechanical system tied directly into the rudder, that works off compass directions," Thomas said. "I set the direction and the autopilot pretty much maintains that heading. Plus, GPS, AIS, and radar are all integrated into the chart plotter. If we drift off course, I'll know it soon enough."

"If it's all electronic, why were you looking at paper charts last night?"

"A little old school, I guess," Thomas said. "I can plot and follow a course on paper, if needed. I just like to be prepared."

"Do you expect any bad weather?" Mickey asked.

"On an extended cruise there's almost always bad weather, especially in the Pacific," Thomas said. "But the boat is more than capable, and we're prepared."

"I think I asked before if someone needs to stay up all night," Mickey said. "I don't remember if you answered."

"Yes and no," Thomas said. "The autopilot will keep us on the right heading and AIS and radar provide collision alarms, so sleeping is possible. But after a day or two I become extremely attuned to the movement of the boat and tend to wake up if something changes. I usually end up making several quick checks nightly."

Mickey made a three-sixty around the horizon and pointed at several dolphins keeping pace off the starboard side. She got Thomas' attention and continued pointing at the dolphins.

Thomas looked in that direction, smiled, and nodded.

"I guess I'll head down below," Mickey said.

"I'll be down in a bit," Thomas said.

Mickey carefully stepped down the ladder, keeping a two-hand hold against the canted angle of the boat in its heeled-over position. She held onto the saloon table as the boat bucked over a wave. "Will it always be this rough?" Mickey asked of Susan, who knelt in front of the open refrigerator.

"This is actually fairly smooth," Susan said. "But it can get rough. You'll get used to the boat's movement after a while. Moving around the boat will get easier."

Mickey kept her grasp on the table as she gazed around the cabin. "If you say so."

Susan glanced back at Mickey and smiled. "Do you want something to drink? You need to stay hydrated."

"I'm okay, for now," Mickey said. "How will we ever be able to prepare meals with all this movement?"

"Like I said, you'll get used to it."

Thomas bounded down the ladder. "Is there any coffee?" he said, as he stepped to the navigation station and began flipping switches. Monitors came to life.

"Coming up," Susan said.

Mickey carefully made her way over to the nav station and held onto the vertical beam that ran from the dividing bulkhead, to the overhead. She examined the monitors as Thomas adjusted knobs. "What's all this?"

Thomas pointed to the largest monitor, with a split screen. "This is the AIS and chart plotter, on the left. The triangle in the middle is us. The other triangles are the other boats around us. The max range for identifying other boats is around twenty miles. This screen displays our course, direction, speed over ground, and depth. It's tied into GPS which, of course, determines our position and calculates our speed." He pointed to the adjacent screen. "I have a low-amp, high-resolution radar system that's good out to about thirty miles." He pointed to other instruments. "This is our VHS radio which we can use to communicate with other boats." He put his finger on a separate instrument. "We also have a Single Side-Band radio for long-distance communication. And I always carry a sat phone. The rest of this stuff has to do with the operation of the boat. I can see the status of our batteries from here, the percent of charge, what's going out, and what's coming in from the solar panels, the wind turbine, and such. This monitor will also show the power input from the engine or generator, when they are running. The water maker uses a fair amount of power so I use the engine or generator for that process. I can even monitor the temperature of the refrigerator. Most of the navigation and communication equipment is duplicated up at the helm. We actually tend to spend most of our time in the cockpit. Electronics are great, and make for a much more comfortable cruise, but keeping physical watch as much as possible is still important. Of course, I have backups for most of the equipment, including the autopilot."

Mickey shook her head back and forth. "Wow. This all seems really complicated."

"At first," Thomas said. "I'll show you how this stuff works once we settle into a routine."

"I'd like that," Mickey said.

Susan shuffled some pots around and closed the locker. "We need to run through the safety equipment with Mickey."

Thomas nodded. "No time like the present." He looked at Mickey. "Have you decided which berth you'll be in?"

"I guess I'll try the lower bunk in the middle cabin," Mickey said. "It's closer to the bathroom."

"Head," Thomas corrected.

Mickey smiled. "Sorry—head."

Thomas stood up and started forward. "Follow me."

Mickey fell in behind and followed him into the middle cabin.

He opened a locker, pulled out a life jacket, and handed it to Mickey. "Let's start with this and how to put it on."

***

Thomas had just finished pointing out the fire extinguishers onboard when Susan called for lunch. Susan was grabbing three bottles of beer from the fridge when Thomas and Mickey stepped back into the saloon.

Mickey peered at the sandwiches and potato salad on three plates. "I could have helped with that."

"You'll have plenty of opportunity," Susan said. "This is our first meal aboard. I thought a beer was in order, to celebrate."

"Let's take this up to the cockpit," Thomas said, as he grabbed a plate and a beer, and headed for the ladder. He used an elbow against a bulkhead to steady himself as he sprang up the ladder.

Susan handed the two remaining bottles to Mickey. "Take these up and then I'll hand you the plates."

Mickey held the bottles in one hand as she stepped up the ladder. She placed both bottles in bottle holders and then turned back to the hatch, where she took the two plates from Susan.

Thomas scanned the horizons until Susan and Mickey found seats and got comfortable with the boat's motion.

Thomas held his beer in the air. "Here's to a joyous voyage."

Susan and Mickey motioned with their bottles and then took a swig.

The three of them ate, drank, and talked, mostly about the boat and what to expect on the water.

Mickey heard a *beep* and saw Thomas glance at the chart plotter on the nav pod. He then scanned the ocean off the port bow. Mickey looked in that direction and saw a large boat in the distance, just a speck. "What does the beep mean?"

"According to the chart plotter, our course will intersect the course of that tanker," he pointed to the horizon.

"Do we need to change course?" Susan asked.

Thomas glanced up at the sails and then back to Susan. "If nothing changes, we'll pass their stern with plenty of room to spare. But I probably should trim the sails a little." He glanced back at the main sail. "After lunch." He resumed eating.

"Can you show me how to do it?" Mickey asked. "How you would do it if the electric was out?"

Thomas nodded while chewing. He swallowed. "Glad to." He took another bite.

While Thomas and Susan talked about reorganizing the aft cabin, Mickey gazed out to the horizon. She saw the tanker in the distance, a little larger than before, but the rest of the ocean was empty of manmade objects. The water was relatively smooth, and the boat was able to slice through the surface with little motion, except for those occasions when a gust of wind would cause the boat to heel over a little more.

Mickey enjoyed the wind through her hair and the warmth of the sun. The coach roof provided complete shade where she and Susan sat. Thomas sat directly in the sun. She wondered why the coach roof didn't extend back and completely cover the helm. She then realized that complete coverage of the cockpit would block the view of the sails from the helm. An unobstructed view of the sails was important in order to keep them trimmed.

She thought about her last conversation with Jack, at the office the morning before she left for California. He seemed genuinely sorry, but then, this was not the first of his dalliances. And it was not the first time he was sorry for what he had done. On the other hand, she got along great with Jack. He was smart, handsome, and funny. He made her laugh, which her might be the best quality in a man. She had only been gone a couple of days and she missed him already. She regretted not calling him the previous night, or this morning before she boarded the boat. But that's water under the keel, so to speak, and she would never ask to use Thomas' sat phone to talk with Jack. She would give him a call when the boat reached Hawaii. In the meantime, back to the sun, wind, ocean spray, and the company of her family.

"Want to give me a hand with the sails," Thomas said.

Mickey brought her attention back to the cockpit. "Absolutely."

Thomas stood, opened a locker in the cockpit, and retrieved a shiny steel handle. "Winch handle, if we were to need it." He put the handle back in the locker. "Most of the winches have a handle nearby." He then motioned Mickey closer and pointed to each of the winches around the cockpit, and their corresponding lines. He explained how each line was used to reduce and increase the size of the main and jib sails. He then showed her the sheets, the lines used to change the position of the sails to maximize their efficiency against the wind. To illustrate, he wrapped a line around one of the winches and cranked the handle a couple of turns. "If the electric was out, you'd have to hand-crank the winch with the winch handle."

Mickey nodded as she gazed up at the sails. "How do you know if they need to be trimmed?"

"It mostly comes with experience," Thomas said. "But you can use the telltales as a guide, the sails themselves, and how the boat feels."

"The telltales?"

Thomas pointed at the bits of cloth waving in the wind at the edge of the main sail.

Mickey nodded again.

"Given the condition of the water, the wind speed, direction, and our course, the sails are trimmed about as well as possible," Thomas said. "Constant wind, like now, requires fewer adjustments to the boat."

Mickey looked up at the sails again and then off the starboard bow at the immense tanker, which had already passed over their course. It was obvious that the sailboat would pass several hundred yards behind the tanker. She looked back at Thomas. "What do we do if the winds get stronger and the sea rougher?"

"Generally, just reduce sail and keep a sharp watch on everything." Thomas motioned with his finger for Mickey to follow him. "Might as well show you the various aspects of the boat while things are calm." He stepped out of the cockpit and made his way along the deck, being sure to keep a double handhold as he moved along. "If the winds were any stronger, we'd attach ourselves to a jack line, to keep from going over."

Mickey stayed close behind, keeping a tight hold on the various parts of the boat as she moved along.

Thomas shuffled along until he was at the tip of the bow. He bent down and opened a hatch to reveal the anchor chain. He pointed to some buttons. "This lowers the anchor, and this button raises it back up." He pointed to the green garden hose coiled at the bottom of the hold. "I use that to wash any mud off the chain as it comes up. Again, if electric was out the anchor would need to be hand-cranked back up." He put his hand on the winch.

The boat bucked a little as it took the waves in stride.

Mickey tightened her hands around the guardrail until her knuckles were white. She glanced back at Susan, who was watching them from the cockpit.

Thomas stood and made his way along the guardrail. He stopped occasionally to point out various hatches, how they opened, and the various lines and cables. He stopped at the dinghy secured to the deck in front of the mast and explained that it wouldn't be needed in the open ocean. He said that when needed he would use the halyard to lift it over to the water.

Back at the stern he pointed out the various antennas, the solar panels hanging off the port and starboard sides, the wind turbine, and radar.

"I should have showed you all this at the dock," Thomas said. "Just anxious to get started."

Mickey nodded and smiled. She then turned and stepped back into the cockpit.

"How was the tour?" Susan asked.

"Learned a lot," Mickey replied. "Can you operate all this stuff?"

"Not as well as Thomas," Susan said. "But I can do what needs to be done, if needed."

Thomas took a seat next to the helm. "When we first got this boat, we spent a whole day practicing man-overboard drills in open water. Susan did great."

"I could sail this boat if I had to," Susan said.

Thomas stood up and gazed around the horizon. "Speaking of sailing the boat, do you mind if I take a cat nap down below?"

"Go ahead," Susan said. "We girls will be fine up here."

Thomas winked and then disappeared through the hatch.

"He'll probably spend a lot of tonight up here," Susan said.

Mickey watched the wheel as it moved back and forth on its own. "That thing is amazing, must take a lot of the burden."

"It does," Susan said. "Hand steering would be doable with a larger crew, but with just us, the pilot is a necessity. It's so important that Thomas has spare parts, and even a backup system, if needed."

Mickey nodded and then peered at the horizon. She watched a fish leap from the water and then flop back to the surface. "Do you see whales out here?"

"Plenty of them," Susan said.

Mickey picked up the empty lunch plates and beer bottles. "I'll run these below. Want anything?"

"I'm fine."

Mickey made her way down the ladder and placed the dishes in the sink. The boat's movement made standing in one spot a bit of a challenge, but Mickey managed by leaning her hip against the counter top. She ran some water and washed the three plates and forks, dried everything, and put them away. She then returned to the cockpit and took a seat next to Susan.

The two of them talked on, each occasionally checking the horizon, until Mickey noticed the sun beginning to dip in the southwestern sky.

"It's going to be a beautiful sunset," Mickey said.

"Hopefully we'll have clear skies the entire trip," Susan said.

Mickey looked at her and raised an eyebrow. "How likely is that?"

"Not very," Susan said. "But it doesn't hurt to hope."

Mickey nodded and smiled.

CHAPTER 4

Thomas sat at the nav station, examining various instruments, while Mickey and Susan put the finishing touches on dinner.

"Are we eating down here, or up in the cockpit?" Mickey asked, as she moved a pot from the stove.

"I think down here," Thomas said. "Nothing to see up there in the dark."

Susan placed a salmon filet on each of three plates and then added brown rice and steamed vegetables. "It's ready," she said, as she and Mickey moved the plates and glasses of wine to the table.

Thomas flipped a couple of switches and then took a seat at the table. "Looks like the wind will pick up tomorrow, but it shouldn't be too bad. Thirty knots, or so."

"Is there a storm coming?" Mickey asked.

"There's a system well north of us, but nothing for us to worry about."

The three ate and sipped on their wine for an hour or so. While Thomas and Susan continued chatting, Mickey collected the dishes and then washed, dried, and put them away. She then returned to the table.

"More wine?" Mickey asked, as she picked up the bottle.

Thomas put his hand over his empty glass. "Just the one for me, otherwise I'll fall asleep at the helm."

"Will you be up there all night?" Susan asked.

"Yeah, but I should be able to get a few hours of sleep," he said. "I don't expect the wind to pick up until around six. In fact, I might as well head up there now."

"Okay," Susan said. "I need to straighten up a few things, and then I plan to hit the rack early."

Thomas stepped up the ladder, turned back with a smile, and then disappeared through the hatch.

"Will thirty knot winds be serious?" Mickey asked.

"We've been through a lot stronger winds," Susan said. "It'll be a little bumpy, but we'll be fine."

Mickey pursed her lips and made a weak attempt at a smile. "I think I'm too wired up to sleep right now. I think I'll get some pointers from Thomas on night sailing."

"I have some stuff to do in the aft cabin," Susan said. "And then I'm turning in."

They both stood and hugged.

"First of many days on the ocean," Susan said. "I'm really happy you could come along."

"Me, too," Mickey said.

"Do you have everything you need?" Susan asked.

"I'm set," Mickey said. "Don't worry, I'll be fine."

Susan nodded, turned off some lights around the saloon and galley, and then shuffled down the passageway past the nav station.

Mickey washed, dried, and put the wine glasses away, made a three-sixty around the cabin, and then climbed up the ladder.

She emerged into the cockpit and took a seat near the hatch.

Thomas smiled as he removed ear pods, wrapped the wires around an iPod, and set it on the seat next to him. "Not much to see up here at night."

Mickey nodded. "I just wanted to get an idea of what's involved with navigating at night and avoiding objects."

He pointed to the instrument panel. "AIS and radar." He motioned for Mickey to take a look.

She moved to behind the wheel, next to Thomas, and gazed at the iPad-sized screen, split between AIS and radar. There were no black triangles on either screen, except for Roundabout in the middle.

"No traffic out to about thirty miles," Thomas said. He pointed to a spot on the red course line. "Winds should pick up about here."

"What about the sails?" Mickey asked, as she looked up at the white triangles blocking the stars.

"I reduce sails at night," Thomas said. "I'll reduce them more when the wind picks up. Just takes a push of a button. If all goes as expected, we'll be down to a partial jib only by sunrise."

Mickey nodded and glanced at the buttons that controlled the furling of both sails. She folded her arms together and hunched her shoulders to stretch her neck.

"Don't worry," Thomas said.

They continued to chat into the evening. Thomas explained how the autopilot worked and that he had a mechanical Hydrovane as a backup. He pointed to the device on the stern.

"I'll explain how that works when we reach calmer waters, in the daylight."

Mickey nodded.

"So what do you think of your first day at sea?"

"Exciting and a little scary," Mickey said.

"That's good," Thomas said. "You should always be a little scared of the open ocean. Don't take anything for granted. It's important to stay alert and have a backup plan for every contingency."

"Doesn't leave much time to relax," Mickey said.

"You get accustomed to the normal operation of the boat, its feel, sounds, the wind, and waves. It becomes second nature. I'm able to relax and stay attuned at the same time. Plus, I'm on top of anything not working right. Got to keep the boat shipshape."

Mickey nodded, smiled, and then looked around at the dark. "I guess I should turn in."

"I'll see you in the morning," Thomas said.

Mickey stood, stepped through the hatch, and down the ladder. The single night light in the saloon was enough for Mickey to make her way around the table and to the head. She exited the head a few minutes later and then rolled into the lower bunk. She stared into the dark and listened to the creaking of the boat as it maneuvered through the waves. The rocking motion put her at ease and soon she was fast asleep.

***

The boat bucked, nearly tossing Mickey out of her bunk.

She blinked her eyes open and wrapped both hands around the edge of the wall next to her head. She pressed her feet against the opposite wall, thus wedging herself in place. Light from the glass-covered porthole, and the overhead hatch, filled the cabin. Mickey held tight against the violent up-and-down, back-and-forth motion. She soon realized the boat was heeled over way more than before and was taking a pounding against the waves.

Still dressed in the cotton shorts and T-shirt from the day before, she swung her feet to the deck, and stood with both feet planted wide apart. She held onto the upper bunk with both hands, her butt pressed against the vanity, to keep from falling over. The boat bucked again. Both her feet came off the deck an inch or so and then back down with a *whump* as the boat hit the bottom of a trough.

The boat creaked and groaned, barely audible above the waves crashing against the hull and the wind overhead. The double-bunk cabin twisted and canted in one direction, and then immediately in the other direction.

Don't worry, she says. Everything will be fine, she says. Susan's words rattled around in Mickey's brain as she fought to stay upright. Slowly, she got a feel for the tossing and turning, and was able to reach for the door handle with her right hand while holding onto the upper bunk with her left. She twisted the knob. The door flung open. Her fingers wrapped white around the door handle. She shifted her left hand to the door jamb and then stepped through the opening with one foot. She braced her back against the opposite door jamb and looked into the saloon.

Everything gimbaled swung back and forth in unison with the rolling of the boat. The vegetable and fruit baskets hanging near the galley took the motion of the boat in stride. The gimbaled stove rocked back and forth. Pots and pans slid back and forth. But, so far, nothing had spilled to the floor. The saloon and galley looked as it did the day before, except they were moving a lot more.

Since no one could sleep through this and the area was deserted, Mickey figured Thomas and Susan were in the cockpit. Mickey glanced back at the porthole, and then the hatch overhead, and saw water slosh over both.

She stepped back into her cabin, wedged herself between the bunk bed and the vanity, and opened one of the lockers over the top bunk. She retrieved her water and windproof jacket and slipped it on. She then rolled back into the bottom bunk, grabbed her deck shoes, which were tumbled in the opposite corner from where she left them, and slid them on her feet. She then rolled out of the bunk and pulled herself to an upright position.

Mickey eased herself back through the doorway, into the passageway, and through the saloon, finding handholds for both hands as she moved along.

There was less light than normal coming through the main hatch and she realized that the hatch cover was closed, but the door was open.

Mickey climbed the ladder and poked her head through the opening. She saw Thomas and Susan sitting at opposite sides of the wheel. The wheel turned back and forth on its own, obviously under the control of the autopilot.

"Are we in the middle of the storm?" Mickey called out from the hatch.

Thomas and Susan turned their heads in Mickey's direction. Neither looked particularly worried.

"We're on the very edge," Thomas said. "Winds are gusting to around forty knots. We're under reduced sails. The boat is riding just fine."

"Seems a little bumpy to me," Mickey said, as she squeezed through the hatch doors and immediately plopped down next to Susan.

Susan smiled and placed a hand on Mickey's arm as reassurance that all was okay.

Mickey smiled and scanned the ocean. The water was seriously choppy, with an occasional larger wave. The scene was made more ominous because of the gray, overcast skies.

"We should be through this in a couple of hours," Thomas said. "The winds will die down."

Mickey nodded.

"We'll need to wait till then before we can eat breakfast," Susan said.

Breakfast was the last thing on Mickey's mind. Even with her seasickness medicine she was feeling a little dizzy and a bit of nausea. Being up on deck and able to stare out on the ocean helped.

Mickey twisted until she could see over the coach roof. The main was furled away, and the jib wasn't much larger than a t-shirt. The boat was taking the waves in stride and all looked okay to her, given her extremely limited knowledge of sailing a large yacht.

"Are there any other boats nearby?" Mickey asked.

"A couple," Thomas said. "Both moved south of their course to avoid the higher winds of the actual storm. I spoke to both captains over the VHF and I'm keeping an eye on their position on AIS."

Mickey twisted around to get an oblique view of the screen mounted on the nav pod. Thomas pointed at the three triangles, the middle being Roundabout.

Mickey nodded and then sat back against the gunwale. She looked toward the bow and watched the motion of the boat as it cut through the rough water.

Her stomach felt better, the dizziness had subsided, and she was beginning to relax as she fell into the boat's rhythm.

Just as Thomas had said, after a couple of hours the wind abated, the water calmed, and lighter skies appeared ahead.

Thomas pushed some buttons and brought the sails back to their full glory. The boat's speed increased and settled into a slightly heeled over slant.

Susan touched Mickey on the leg. "Let's whip something up for breakfast."

Mickey nodded as she stood and followed Susan.

***

Over the next several days, Mickey fell into a routine. She helped Susan prepare the meals, keep the cabins tidy, and she helped Thomas keep the deck neat and orderly. Thomas usually took a nap for two or three hours in the afternoons down in the aft cabin, weather permitting. Mickey and Susan spent that time in the cockpit, talking over a glass of wine. Thomas spent most nights in the cockpit. He was usually able to sleep there, with only short interruptions. Mickey took every opportunity possible to watch how Thomas handled the boat. She asked a lot of questions. After a while, Thomas trusted her with furling and unfurling the sails, and adjusting the sheets to keep the sails trimmed. Occasionally, he would take the boat off autopilot and let Mickey have a go at the wheel. So far, the voyage had been mostly idyllic, with only a minor squall here and there. They were making good time, slightly ahead of what Thomas projected.

Thomas explained how the AIS identified those boats that carried an AIS transmitter. A beep would sound if Roundabout was projected to intersect the course of such a boat or ship. Mickey had heard the beep numerous times over the previous days. And she was usually able to find the craft on the horizon. But even with AIS it was still important to keep an eye on the radar and on the horizon, since not every boat carried an AIS transmitter.

Most times when the AIS identified other boats and ships in the area, especially sailing craft, Thomas got on the VHF and made contact. Each contact was an opportunity to exchange weather and wind information. Thomas showed Mickey how to find the channels, and how to operate the radio.

At least once a day, weather permitting, Thomas would bring the boat to a complete stop and they would take turns bathing from the transom. For the first couple of days Mickey wore her bikini, but once she realized that Thomas and Susan really paid little attention, she started stripping completely, as Thomas and Susan did.

A few times Mickey jumped in the water, despite her fear of sharks. She was usually in and out in a matter of seconds. But most of the time she would use the stern hose, normally used to wash down the deck.

She'd get wet, then soap down her hair and body, and then rinse. And then a final rinse with fresh water from a bucket.

Thomas tried to keep the fresh water tank topped off, just in case the water maker stopped working.

Late afternoons, before the sun went down, was Mickey's favorite part of the day. That's when everyone gathered for dinner, usually in the cockpit, to watch the sun set.

Breakfast and lunch were simple meals, but Susan tried to make dinner special, with a meat or fish entrée and sides of vegetables and a starch. There was usually dessert of some sort, such as ice cream or pudding. Susan even made a pumpkin pie, knowing it was Mickey's favorite.

Mickey pitched in, which made the days pass quickly.

***

"We just passed the halfway point," Thomas said, looking up from the chart plotter mounted on the cockpit's nav pod.

Mickey leapt up from her seat, eyes wide, to check out the course indicator. "I can't believe we've traveled this far. The days have just flown by."

Despite careful applications of sunblock, Mickey's body had turned a light brown, with resulting bikini lines. The healthy diet, work around the boat, and yoga sessions with Susan made Mickey even leaner than she had been. The very slight abdominal pouch she usually carried was gone, which left her stomach flat. She even had a bit of a six-pack. Her arms and legs were strong and toned from the constant balancing act necessary for life on board an open ocean boat. Her blond hair was a shade or two lighter, which accentuated her deep blue eyes.

She felt at home on the boat and totally relaxed and comfortable around Thomas and Susan, even during bath time.

The only thing she really couldn't get used to was the toilet. It was electric, which worked better than a hand pump system, but the constant motion of the boat made using it somewhat of a chore. It had gotten a little easier, but it certainly wasn't like being home.

That was one of the few things on the boat that made her think of home. The other was Thomas and Susan's relationship. They obviously loved each other. Mickey could not imagine Thomas even looking at another woman, unlike Jack. They were comfortable together, they got along well, and they made each other laugh. Their interaction reminded Mickey of exactly what she didn't have with Jack. Time and distance made that crystal clear. She was even getting used to not having a companion on the boat, which gave her the time and mental freedom to get to know herself. Something her mother used to say often popped into her brain, especially at night just before falling asleep. *If you have yourself as a friend you'll never be lonely.* Mickey didn't really understand it back then, but she was beginning to understand it now.

Thomas stood up and looked to starboard as though something had caught his attention. "We have a boat approaching."

Susan and Mickey turned their heads in unison and both stood up for a better look.

Off in the distance, barely a speck, Mickey saw the white foam of a wake headed in their direction. It was a motor launch large enough to be on the open ocean, and it was moving fast.

"What is it?" Susan asked.

"It's not on AIS, so they are not transmitting a signal," Thomas said.

"What does that mean?" Mickey asked.

"It could mean anything," Thomas said. "But I don't like the looks of it."

CHAPTER 5

"Susan, mind the helm," Thomas said, as he darted across the cockpit and down the hatch.

Mickey followed close behind. "What are you going to do?"

Thomas glanced back as he rounded the corner heading toward the aft cabin. "I think we should open up the arms locker."

Mickey stopped dead in her tracks. Her mouth gaped open while she thought about what that might mean. She had never even asked about whether Thomas had a gun on board. It didn't enter her mind. She presumed the only thing they had to worry about was the wind and the sea. But Thomas' words brought her back to the simple fact that no matter where people traveled, they were never far from potential violence. But out here, on the ocean, alone, made people like Thomas, Susan, and Mickey easy prey.

Mickey had never fired a gun, much less owned one. Owning a gun in New York City was a major pain, and Mickey never thought it necessary to possess a gun, despite all the violence reported in the news. She thought about it. She and Jack even discussed it. But in the end it was all a lot of trouble, with a steep learning curve. She was surprised Thomas, as a resident of California, owned a gun. California made gun ownership even more of a pain.

Mickey continued around the corner into the aft cabin and found Thomas standing in the middle of the double bed. He opened a metal cabinet affixed to the bulkhead high up, next to the overhead. He turned a key and swung the door open. Inside, Mickey saw a rifle, two handguns, and boxes of ammunition. Thomas retrieved the rifle and one of the handguns.

"Did you ever learn how to shoot?" Thomas said, looking at Mickey.

"No, does Susan?"

"Absolutely," Thomas said. "We both took the necessary classes and we go to the range as often as possible." He held up the handgun. "She's a regular Johnny Ringo with this Glock." He reached back into the locker and grabbed extra magazines for both weapons and then stepped down to the deck. He placed everything on the bed and then picked up the rifle. He pulled back the slide, looked into the chamber, and then let the slide slam forward. "Ruger Mini-14 ranch rifle, but it works just as good on the ocean." He put the rifle down, picked up the pistol, pulled the slide back, and then let it slam forward. He then grabbed the rifle and an extra magazine and darted out of the cabin.

Mickey followed him up the ladder and back into the cockpit.

"Any changes?" he asked Susan.

"They're still headed this way," Susan said.

Thomas handed the Glock to Susan and then laid his rifle on the seat next to the wheel. He picked up the VHF radio handset, adjusted a dial, and spoke. "Motor craft approaching sailing yacht, please state your intentions." The radio came back with static. Thomas repeated the same message, and then again.

Mickey looked at the approaching boat, but saw no change in their direction or speed. She sat next to Susan and took hold of her arm. Lines of tension etched her face. "I don't mind telling you, I'm getting a little worried."

Susan glanced at her, gave a weak smile, and then nodded. She then turned her attention back to Thomas. "Should we lower the sails and use the engine?"

Thomas opened a locker and took out a pair of binoculars. He peered through the lenses. "There's no one visible on deck. No sign of weapons. Let's maintain our speed and course and see what they do.

The motor launch turned and fell in behind Roundabout, directly on the stern, but slowed and kept a three or four hundred yard gap between the two boats.

Mickey saw a flash of light from the motor boat and figured it was probably a reflection off the windshield.

Thomas took another look through the binoculars. "Still no one on deck." He then handed the binoculars to Susan and picked up the rifle. He stood facing the stern with the rifle across his chest. Mickey didn't know if letting them see the weapons on board was a good or bad idea.

After a few minutes of matching Roundabout's course and speed, the motor launch finally peeled off, and accelerated heading due south, perpendicular to Roundabout's course.

"What do you think?" Susan asked.

"I think we keep an eye on them until they're out of sight," Thomas said.

Mickey stood and moved over next to Thomas. "It will be dark in a couple of hours, what about tonight?"

Susan stood up. "Yeah, they could move out of radar distance, wait for dark, and then move back in."

Thomas turned his head and stared at Susan. Without saying anything he nodded his head.

"What if they come at us in the dark?" Mickey asked.

Thomas rubbed his chin with his free hand. "Might be a good idea to change course for a while."

"Do we go north or south?" Susan asked.

"We wait until they are off the radar, and then I think we need to steer northwest. If we go south at all, they might run into us accidentally."

Mickey turned to look at the radar screen. She pointed at a blip. "Is that them?"

Thomas glanced over. "Yeah, they're still heading due south. We maintain this course until they are off the screen."

"How long will that take?" Mickey asked.

"Maybe an hour or so," Thomas said. "Then we make our turn."

Mickey watched the radar screen and the blip's steady trek to the south, away from Roundabout's westerly course.

An hour later the blip blinked a couple of times and then disappeared from the edge of the screen.

At dusk, Thomas would normally turn the running lights on, including the one at the top of the mast. But as the sun sunk below the horizon, he jibed to the northwest without the lights.

The wind turned from a broad reach on the port side to a broad reach to starboard.

Thomas adjusted the main and jib sheets and carefully allowed the boom to swing across the stern. Thomas secured the boom with a preventer line, to keep it from swinging back should the wind shift.

Mickey checked the speed indicator. The boat maintained its speed and continued to slice through the water at a good clip. "How long do we stay on this course?"

"Through the night," Thomas said. "If nothing's on the radar in the morning, we'll correct our course for Hilo."

Mickey nodded and then took a seat next to Susan. "Is it safe to run without lights?" Mickey asked.

"Not ideal," Susan said. "But Thomas will keep a sharp eye on the radar and AIS." She placed a hand on Mickey's shoulder. "Let's go down and whip something up for dinner before the sun goes completely down. Sandwiches, I think."

Mickey nodded and followed Susan below.

***

Dinner consisted of sandwiches in the cockpit, with only the screens on the nav pod for light. When everyone finished eating, Mickey took the plates down to the galley and placed them in the sink. She then returned to the cockpit and took a seat next to Susan.

"There's no sense in all of us staying up," Susan said. She turned to Mickey. "If you'll stay up here with Thomas, I'll go down and try to get some sleep. I'll relieve you around one or so."

Mickey and Thomas nodded.

Susan made her way through the hatch and down the ladder.

Mickey moved closer to the wheel. "If you want to try to get some sleep, I can keep watch. I'll wake you if anything changes."

Thomas rubbed the whiskers on his chin and then nodded. "Wake me if anything changes, or doesn't feel right."

"Count on it," Mickey said.

Thomas reduced the sail on the main and jib, and then tweaked the trim on both. He checked the course and made a slight adjustment to the autopilot heading. He looked at Mickey, raised his chin, and then reclined full-length on the port side teak settee, with his head near the helm. He closed his eyes and within a few minutes he was snoring softly.

Mickey wished she could fall asleep like that. She was one of those who could not sleep unless her accommodations were close to perfect. Which meant, she couldn't sleep on an airplane. It took a while to get used to sleeping on the boat, but at least she was able to lie flat.

She checked the chart plotter, wind speed, direction, and the boat's speed. Reducing the sails had dropped their speed to just under three knots. The sea was calm and the westerly wind was steady. She did a slow three-sixty of the open ocean. All was dark; no lights in any direction.

She finally sat down in the helmsman's seat and listened to the water against the boat and an occasional flap of the sail. Minor gusts gently heeled the boat over an extra degree or two. Mickey felt like she was on a porch swing with a warm breeze tickling the hair against the back of her neck.

Her mind wandered back to Jack. He was an asshole, she knew, but she also knew that she missed him. She couldn't help it. She wondered if it was a good idea to be gone so long. There was no telling what he was doing in her absence. She wondered about work, and whether the new account was being handled the way she had promised the company's leadership.

An indicator on the AIS screen brought her out of her reverie. She stood and examined the screen, which now indicated one other boat within range of Roundabout's receiver. The extra triangle was well off Roundabout's starboard bow, heading west. Mickey wondered why the alarm did not sound, but quickly realized the course of the two boats was not projected to cross.

She pressed on the screen which brought up the boat's, actually a ship, a large cargo ship, identification. The screen provided the ship's name, size, destination, and VHF channel. She figured it probably originated in Asia somewhere, heading to the States full of stuff, more stuff for Americans to consume.

She thought about the crew on such a large vessel, and what they did on board hour to hour, day to day. She wondered about their sleeping quarters, what must be a large galley, and the food they ate. Compared to Roundabout, the cargo ship must be a floating city.

Mickey checked roundabout's course and speed. Nothing had changed, so she resumed her position in the helmsman's seat. She looked over at the dark blob of Thomas' body, still on his back with his head to one side, snoring. Louder now. She wondered how Susan was able to sleep next to that kind of noise. Mickey preferred total quiet, which was lacking on an ocean-going vessel the size of Roundabout. But after a few days she got used to the banging, and creaking, and flapping, along with the rocking, and occasional tossing about. Susan was right, this was an adventure. One Mickey would remember the rest of her life.

Time passed slowly. Mickey was left to her own thoughts until a little before one, when Susan emerged from the hatch.

She shuffled over and took a seat next to Mickey. "Has he been asleep the whole time?" she asked in a low voice.

"Yep," Mickey said. She pointed to the nav pod. "We're still on Thomas' last course, doing a little less than three knots. Not a lot of flapping from the sails, so they must be trimmed fairly well."

Susan's chin nodded up and down, lit up red and green from the instrument displays. "You should get some sleep," Susan said. "I'll let Thomas sleep as much as possible."

Mickey nodded, stood up, and placed a hand on Susan's shoulder, before she ambled to the hatch, and down the ladder. She made her way through the saloon, to the head. She came out a few minutes later, crossed the passage way, and rolled into her bottom bunk.

The boat's gentle rocking and relative quiet soon had her fast asleep.

***

The next morning Mickey, wearing her usual bikini top, shorts, and deck shoes, came up from below to find Thomas behind the helm and Susan asleep on the teak settee. "Anything on the horizon?" Mickey whispered.

Thomas shook his head. "Nope, all is clear. I resumed our original course to Hilo and raised the sails a few minutes ago."

Mickey glanced at the instruments and saw that Roundabout was doing just over five knots.

Susan rolled her head toward Mickey and blinked her eyes open. "Any sign of the pirates?"

"Nope," Thomas said.

She swung her feet to the deck and stretched her back. "Even with the cushion, this bench is not all that comfortable."

"I appreciate you both being up here last night," Thomas said.

Mickey nodded.

Susan got to her feet. "I'm in the mood for a substantial breakfast. How do eggs, bacon, and toast sound?"

"Sounds yummy," Thomas said, as he glanced at the sails and checked the nav pod instruments.

Mickey headed to the hatch, followed by Susan.

"Mickey, could you stay up on deck a few minutes and help with the spinnaker? We're pretty much down wind and the winds are light enough."

Mickey stopped and turned back into the cockpit. "Sure."

Susan continued down the ladder.

Mickey had watched Thomas and Susan go through the process several times and had actually taken over for Susan the last few times. At this point she felt confident with her part of raising the spinnaker, as long as there were no problems.

With the autopilot off, Mickey kept the helm steady while under power from the main and jib, and watched Thomas make his way forward.

He retrieved the bag containing the large asymmetrical sail and carried it to the bow. He opened the bag and hooked the sail's head to the spinnaker halyard, while standing on the windward side of the jib. He then searched through the bag for the tack and clew, the corners, and attached the necessary lines.

Mickey took up the slack on the lines at Thomas' direction and then secured the lines.

Thomas hoisted the spinnaker, still in the sock, to the top of the mast and then adjusted the mass so it would not foul with the jib. He then pulled on a line which raised the sock, allowing the bright blue spinnaker to billow out.

With the spinnaker full of air, Mickey furled the jib.

Thomas hustled back to the cockpit and adjusted the sheet lines so the spinnaker was at its maximum efficiency.

"Good job," Thomas said, as he turned to Mickey and smiled.

"Next time you'll have to show me how to do your part," Mickey said, as she glanced at the speed indicator. The speed over ground had increased to almost nine knots.

Thomas set the course on the autopilot, activated the system, and took a seat behind the wheel. "It's fairly straight forward. You could probably do it without me showing you."

Mickey took a final look at the instruments, especially the AIS, which indicated there were no vessels in range. She looked at the large blue sail and at the foam in the water as the boat cut through the relatively calm surface. "We've been lucky with the lack of storms."

"We have," Thomas said. "It's a good time of the year to cross. The trade winds are favorable. The low pressure cell, so far, has kept itself to the north, which means we didn't have to go too far south to catch the westerlies."

Mickey glanced at the rifle and pistol still on the bench next to Thomas. "Is it a problem taking guns into different jurisdictions, especially foreign countries?"

"It's a major pain," Thomas said, "if they know about them." He smiled and raised an eyebrow.

Mickey nodded, took another look around at the shimmering ocean, and then turned to the hatch. "I'll give Susan a hand."

Breakfast consisted of scrambled eggs with cheese, pancakes with maple syrup, sausage links, orange juice, and coffee, all enjoyed at the cockpit table along with sunshine, a steady breeze, and the dark blue ocean around them.

There was no rush to get anything done. The mood by everyone was relaxed.

The spinnaker pulled the boat along at eight to nine knots as though there was not a care in the world.

CHAPTER 6

Thomas used the spinnaker when the winds were right, the main and jib when the winds were higher, and the motor when the winds were nonexistent. Overall, they made good time with mostly favorable winds, no serious storms, and no further threats from potential pirates. Day to day, they followed their established routines, taking turns at the helm, preparing meals, and general boat maintenance. Mickey grew more and more confident at the helm and handling the sails. She usually used the electric wenches to raise, lower, and position the sails, but on occasion, when she felt the need for more exercise, she'd use the hand crank on the winches.

The twelfth day of the voyage brought more sunshine and good winds. Thomas stood at the helm, alone in the cockpit. Susan and Mickey were below, preparing lunch.

"You guys may want to see this," Thomas called out.

Susan and Mickey came through the hatch and stepped into the cockpit.

Susan looked around the cockpit. "What?"

Thomas pointed toward the bow. "Mauna Loa and Mauna Kea just visible over the horizon."

Susan and Mickey turned in unison.

Mickey could just make out the hazy protrusions above the horizon in the far off distance. "How far are they?"

Thomas glanced at the chart plotter. "We're sixteen miles out, about two-and-a-half hours."

Susan turned to the hatch. "Let's finish lunch, eat, and then start getting ready to spend a night or two in a real hotel room."

"A real shower," Mickey said, as she turned to follow Susan. "And a bed that doesn't move."

They ate lunch in the cockpit and watched as the island grew larger.

Susan turned to Mickey. "Are you leaving us?"

Mickey raised both eyebrows, exhaled, and paused. Her intention was to leave the boat in Hilo and fly back to New York. The twelve days at sea had been good, great really. If Thomas and Susan were heading back, she'd make the return trip for sure. But they were heading farther south, to Samoa, and probably on to Fiji. Round trip, they would be gone two months or more. Mickey had not intended to be gone that long. It would be possible, though, to continue on and then fly back from Samoa. That would mean she'd be gone for at least a full month; not that long really. But there was Jack. The separation had been good. It had given her time to think about something besides Jack, and the office, and work. She had not taken a real vacation in years. But would she have a job if she stayed gone two months, or even one month? There was a lot up in the air. "I told the office I was going to Hilo."

"Is there a pressing reason why you need to get back?" Thomas asked. "We'll miss your company. And the South Pacific is where the adventures really begin."

"It's only another fifteen days or so," Susan said. "You can fly back from there if you want."

"Let me sleep on it," Mickey said. "But either way, I need to wash every piece of clothing I have and take a long hot shower."

Susan nodded. "We'll check in, have a nice dinner, and do all the other stuff tomorrow. We usually stay at the Seaside Hotel. It's close, nice, and they have all the facilities we'll need. Plus there's a really nice restaurant next door. It's called Fronds. They have fine American dining. You'll love it."

Mickey smiled, nodded, and looked toward the approaching island.

***

With the sails lowered, Thomas radioed ahead and then motored the boat into the Hilo Harbor Basin, rounded the seawall to port, and followed it into Radio Bay.

Susan stood at the bow, ready to position the fenders.

Mickey stood next to Thomas in the cockpit and watched him as he maneuvered the boat for docking.

"No fuel at the dock," Thomas said. "I'll need to call for a truck delivery. We went through the same process two years ago."

Mickey nodded.

"I'll be putting the port side against the dock," Thomas yelled to Susan.

Susan lowered the fenders into position.

Thomas nodded for Mickey to put the fender out on the port stern.

Thomas turned at the end of a row of yachts, three monohulls and two cats, cut the engine, and let the boat drift to the dock.

"You timed it perfectly," Mickey said.

Thomas nodded.

With the boat next to the dock, Susan climbed out, secured the bow line, and then walked back toward the stern. Thomas tossed her the stern line, which she secured to a cleat.

Thomas grabbed his cell phone from a locker and dialed.

Susan climbed back into the boat and led Mickey below. "We might as well take our laundry and what we're wearing tonight. After Thomas gets the boat fueled and watered, and we get checked in at Customs, we'll call for an Uber for a ride to the hotel."

***

Thomas, Susan, and Mickey sat facing the water as the waiter poured wine. Thomas lifted his glass. "To adventure, family, and many years of the same."

They clinked their glasses and sipped.

"I'm just happy for the hot shower and the shampoo," Mickey said. "My hair needed it."

Susan lowered her glass and picked up the menu. "What are you guys having?"

"Steak, I think," Mickey said. "With little red potatoes and green beans." She looked up. "Do they have that here?"

"They do," Thomas said. "Get the Kobe steak."

Mickey found Kobe steak on the menu. "That much for steak?"

"You're on vacation," Susan said. "Splurge a little. Besides, Thomas is buying."

"No way," Mickey said. "Dinner is on me, and I insist."

"I'm still having the Kobe steak," Thomas said. He smiled.

"The least I could do," Mickey said.

The waiter came, took their orders, and left.

Mickey took a sip of the wine. "Tell me about your trip south."

Thomas explained the course, how they would be crossing the equator, and that he'd be taking some extra diesel just in case, to deal with areas with no wind. He talked about American Samoa, and Fiji, and all the other islands in the area. Plenty of the islands were completely deserted, and he planned to do some exploring, he said.

Mickey listened and thought about how fast the last twelve days had gone by. Once she got her sea legs she really enjoyed being on the boat, the freedom, and the idea that they could go anywhere. She enjoyed learning how to operate the boat. Thomas had taught her a lot about sailing. She thought about maybe having her own boat one day.

The steaks came, and they talked, ate, and drank late into the night. The hotel was nearby, and it only took a few minutes to walk the distance. Mickey had taken a separate room since she thought Thomas and Susan might like to have some time truly alone. They agreed to meet for breakfast at nine, hugged, and then went off to their separate rooms.

Twelve at night in Hawaii meant it was only six in the morning in New York, too early to call. Mickey promised herself to get up early and call Janet first thing.

Inside her room, Mickey slipped out of her sun dress, spent a few minutes in the bathroom, and then crawled into bed.

***

"Hi Janet," Mickey said into her cell phone.

"Mickey, I was wondering when we would hear from you. How was your voyage?"

"It was beautiful, adventurous, and a little scary, all rolled into one. I have had a great time."

"When will you be back?" Janet asked. "Jack has asked about you every day."

"Speaking of Jack," Mickey said, "how is the campaign?"

"The design work is well on its way to being done, Jack has lined up the talent, and they should be ready to shoot as soon as the scripts are written. Jack was hoping you would be back to supervise the writing."

Mickey paced back and forth on the carpeted floor of her room. "I intended to fly back when we reached Hilo, but I'm considering pressing on with

Susan and Thomas for the next leg to Samoa. It will only add another two weeks or so to my trip. I can fly back from there."

There was a pause of several seconds before Janet responded. "You certainly deserve the time off considering what you've done for the company over the past years." There was another pause.

"But?"

"Well, Jack can supervise the writing, but he was hoping you would be returning soon. I think it's more personal that professional."

"I know," Mickey said. "I didn't leave under the best of conditions in that department."

"I figured," Janet said. Janet let out a deep exhale. "Do you intend to speak with him before you head out?"

"This time was different, Janet. I think I need more time away."

"Do what you need to, Mickey," Janet said. "This place will survive. Barely. It's not the same with you gone."

Mickey sat on the edge of the bed. "It's nice to be missed."

"I'll let him know you'll be gone for another two weeks or so. You be careful, and call when you get to Samoa. If I don't hear from you in a couple of weeks, I'll start to worry."

"No need to worry. The boat is solid, and Thomas is very experienced with all kinds of seas. Plus, I'm learning a lot. I may have to think about getting my own boat."

Janet laughed. "You'll have to take me out. I love the water."

"Thanks, Janet. We'll talk soon."

"Take care," Janet said, and then hung up.

Mickey fell back flat on the bed and stared at the ceiling. Mickey loved the voyage, but she was also starting to miss home and her work. She felt bad about signing a new client and then disappearing. But she also felt she needed more time away. More time away from Jack.

She turned her head and looked at the bedside clock. *Seven*. Mickey rolled on her side and closed her eyes.

***

While Thomas stayed behind to take care of minor repairs on the boat, Susan and Mickey called for an Uber and then waited in front of the hotel entrance.

Susan turned to Mickey and smiled. "I'm so happy you decided to continue on. You'll love it in the islands."

Mickey nodded and smiled. "I'm getting used to the boat, even the head," Mickey laughed.

"It's good to see you laugh," Susan said.

The car arrived, and they piled into the small back seat.

"You're going to need some snorkeling equipment," Susan said. She leaned over the front seat. "Is there a dive shop on the way?"

The driver, a young man, thought for a moment. "There is."

"Just drop us there," Susan said. She leaned back and turned to Mickey. "We need to get you some fins, a mask, and snorkel."

"Do I need a wet suit?"

"We can look," Susan said. "Not really necessary unless you scuba deeper, but it would also keep the sun off your back for snorkeling."

"And after the dive shop?"

"We need to restock our food," Susan said. "Do you need any more clothes, or anything?"

"Maybe a couple of more pairs of shorts."

They both laughed and continued talking about what all they needed to get. At the dive shop Mickey picked out the snorkeling equipment, but decided to pass on the wet suit. She didn't intend to do any diving. She wasn't qualified. But she did pick out a new bikini.

Then it was on to Sam's Club where they replenished their food stores, wine, beer, and water. With another Uber loaded down, they returned to the boat.

At the boat, they hauled their provisions on board and stowed everything away. When done, Mickey glistened with perspiration.

"One more night in the hotel was a great idea," Mickey said. "I can't wait for that shower."

"We'll need to be up and out early," Susan said. "But tonight, we head out for another nice dinner. Thomas and I know of a fantastic place."

"We still need to do the laundry," Mickey said.

Susan nodded and then they found Thomas on deck. "You almost done?" Susan asked.

"Need to replace the head sail furling line, and one or two other items," Thomas said. "A couple of more hours. I'll meet you at the hotel."

"We'll see you there," Susan said, as she and Mickey stepped on the dock.

CHAPTER 7

Mickey took a moment to enjoy the early morning. She didn't often get up before the sun, but Thomas wanted to get an early start. She thought about the hot shower she had taken that morning, and how it would be the last for a while. For the next couple of weeks, showers would consist of hosing off with salt water and then a bucket rinse of cold fresh water. She didn't mind the sacrifice. Paradise was worth it.

Mickey pushed the boat away with her foot and then jumped aboard.

Thomas shifted the idling motor into forward and eased the boat away from the dock. He steered along the seawall and then entered the open ocean.

Mickey shuffled along the deck and jumped into the cockpit. She turned and stared at the big island coast to their stern, and then to starboard as Thomas turned east to follow the coast farther south. When they were well off the coast, he raised the main and headsails, and trimmed them to take advantage of the steady westerly fourteen-knot wind. At the southernmost point of the island, aptly named South Point, Thomas steered southwest. There was no weather forecasted, the sun was against a blue sky, and the winds were steady for a near perfect broad reach.

"Let's hoist the spinnaker and see if we can shave a few hours off our voyage," Thomas said to Mickey.

Mickey smiled, nodded, and then carefully made her way along the deck to the bow, where she pulled the sock-covered spinnaker from its locker. She fastened the head, clew, and tack corners, and pulled the halyard until the head was at the top of the mast. She looked back at Thomas to make sure he was ready. When he nodded, Mickey pulled on a line to raise the sock and free the sail. The colorful spinnaker immediately took the wind and blossomed.

Thomas furled the jib and repositioned the main.

Mickey took a final look at the sails and their respective lines and then hurried back to the cockpit. She immediately glanced at the nav pod instruments. "Looks like we gained two-and-a-half knots or so."

"Yep," Thomas said. "If we could maintain this speed we'd be there in record time. Unfortunately, we won't be able to maintain this speed, so we're still looking at two weeks, maybe a little less."

"Fine by me," Mickey said, as she took a seat near Thomas. "Any traffic?" she asked, as she scanned the open ocean.

"Plenty," Thomas said, "but none that will cause us any problems."

Mickey watched the wheel spin on its own, under the control of the autopilot. She checked the sails, and then the chart plotter and the AIS triangles that represented other vessels. Satisfied that she understood where they were and where they were headed, she made a final scan of the ocean, and then stood. "I'll check on Susan."

Thomas looked up from his iPad and nodded.

Mickey made her way across the cockpit and down the hatch.

She found Susan making notes on a piece of paper. She looked up when Mickey entered the saloon. "I'm trying to plan our meals for the next few days."

Mickey nodded as she shuffled up to Susan. "What can I do?"

Susan nodded toward several plastic bags full of food. "Those need to be stowed in the lockers."

Mickey began sorting the cans and bags of dry goods and then found places for them in the various lockers. "You met Jack that one time, what did you think of him?" Mickey asked, as she continued working.

Susan stopped writing and looked up. She paused for several seconds before answering. "Depends on whether you intend to stay with him."

Mickey stopped with a bag of rice in her hand mid-air and cocked her head slightly.

"If you intend to stay with him, he's fine," Susan said. "If you intend to go your own way, I think you're making a good decision."

"Really?"

Susan nodded. "The only person he loves is himself."

"And you got that from just the one meeting?"

"Uh-huh," Susan said, and then turned back to her scribbling.

Mickey paused for a moment, staring at Susan, and then continued with stowing the food. She thought about Jack, their dinners together, weekends away, and the sex. They were all good. But obviously Susan was right. Mickey let out a deep exhale and then reconciled herself to not think about Jack, or work, or New York as long as she was on the boat. "So what do you have planned for dinner?"

***

The next five days and nights were fairly uneventful. The winds were moderate, and the boat made good time. They passed through two squalls, during which the winds reached thirty knots. The first was at night. Mickey watched as Thomas kept the boat under tight control.

For the second squall, which was during the day, Thomas suggested Mickey take the helm. He kept a close eye while she went through the storm procedures, reefed the sails, and steered according to the wind and waves. Salt spray whipped through the cockpit, the bow dipped low in the water, and the boat heeled, but she pressed through with minimal directions from Thomas.

With the storm behind them, she glanced back at the dark clouds, and then at Thomas.

He nodded and winked.

She knew that handling a large boat in a storm was a serious matter. She felt a sense of deep pride that she was able to keep the boat above the surface.

After breakfast on the sixth morning, when the dishes were put away, it was all hands on deck to help Thomas pull in a large Dorado, also referred to as Dolphin and Mahi-Mahi. The fish had hooked himself onto the line that trailed behind Roundabout most of the time. They had been lucky enough to catch several of the fish during the voyage, but this was the largest.

Thomas had to work at reeling the struggling fish to the boat.

Mickey tried several times to gaff him, but each time he dodged the sharp hook.

Thomas finally had Mickey and Susan hold the rod while he took over the gaff. Together they were able to keep the fish near the stern.

With one swift motion, Thomas hooked the fish just behind its gill and jerked him to the deck. The fish flapped for all it was worth until Thomas was able to pin him with a foot. He quickly grabbed a bottle of alcohol from a nearby locker, twisted the top, and poured some into the fish's gill.

Mickey watched with a confused expression. She had never actually watched the process once the fish was on deck; she was usually down below, or busy with something.

"It kills the fish in seconds," Thomas said.

With the fish finally motionless, Thomas unhooked the gaff, the line's hook, and then tied a piece of rope around its tail. Thomas looped the rope around a hand scale and read the weight. "Eighteen pounds. I'll have to make a log entry on this one."

As Mickey watched, Thomas and Susan proceeded to carve up the fish. Thomas filleted both flanks and then cut the fillets into edible portions.

Susan used a second fillet knife to remove the skin from each piece and then put the pieces in a zip-lock bag. "Most will go in the freezer, but looks like dinner is decided." With all the fish sealed in bags, Susan carried them below.

Mickey used the stern hose to wash the fish remains off the deck and into the ocean. She then turned to the helm. "Mind if I practice my manual steering?"

"No prob," Thomas said, as he went about returning utensils to their stowage location and organizing the cockpit.

Mickey took hold of the wheel, turned the autopilot off, and checked the boat's progress along the course line indicated on the chart plotter.

Manually working the wheel was a bit of a workout for Mickey. The muscles in her arms, back, and abdomen flexed as she kept control of the wheel.

"You're looking awfully buff," Susan said, as she returned to the cockpit.

"I miss my workouts back on land," Mickey said. "But operating this boat is as much a workout, probably more."

Susan smiled as she took a seat on the settee.

Thomas went forward and checked the various lines and halyards.

"What's he doing?" Mickey asked.

Susan glanced at Thomas at the bow. "As the lines age, they become more prone to breaking. He checks for any fraying. Doesn't want a line to break while he's trying to reduce sail."

Mickey nodded and then checked her instruments. AIS indicated no boats in range, and radar confirmed that finding. "We're pretty much alone out here."

"Nice, isn't it?" Susan said. "The sun, the sky, the wind, the water, and us. Surrounded by the blue."

Mickey smiled, nodded, and raised an eyebrow. "It is nice. Relaxing. It makes me wonder why we work so hard."

"Money," Susan said. "Can't do this without some money. And not just for the boat."

Mickey raised her chin.

"Something's always breaking," Susan said. "Luckily, Thomas is able to fix pretty much anything on this boat. But it's still expensive to keep it in good shape. You don't want to come out here with anything less."

Mickey nodded.

"And then there's the mooring fees and provisioning at every port. All populated islands have their fees."

"Ever think about living on a boat?" Mickey asked.

"All the time," Susan said. "We've considered it seriously. Maybe some day."

The Mahi caught in the morning made dinner a special event. Susan made coconut rice while Mickey steamed the last of their fresh vegetables. She also put a fruit salad together with the last of their grapes, pineapple, and mango. She crumbled a little feta cheese on the fruit.

While Susan set up the table, Thomas and Mickey doused the spinnaker, and unfurled the jib.

"Let's leave them at full sail for now," Thomas said. "I may reduce them later tonight." He made a last check of the autopilot, AIS, radar, and their course and speed. He and Mickey then went below for dinner.

"This is beautiful," Mickey said, as she reached the bottom of the ladder. "Even a table cloth."

Susan smiled as she moved a bottle of wine to the table and motioned for everyone to take a seat.

For the next two hours the three of them ate, drank, talked, and laughed. Susan told a story about a nine-year-old Mickey always finding the cookies their mother hid.

Finally, Mickey stretched and yawned. "I'm bushed. This was a wonderful day, and I just want to thank you two for inviting me along for the second leg."

"Our pleasure," Thomas said, as he raised his wine glass. "Here's to family."

Glasses clinked, and they drained the last of their wine.

"Let's get this mess cleaned up, and then I need to get some sleep before my shift," Susan said.

"Me, too," Mickey said.

Thomas stood and headed for the hatch. "Suz, I'll see you in a few hours," he said, as he stepped up the ladder.

Susan and Mickey cleaned up the galley, turned out the lights, and shuffled to their respective berths.

As the boat gently rocked Mickey to sleep, she thought of the day, and that there was no reason why there shouldn't be many more like it. She hoped Thomas and Susan actually did end up living on a boat. Soon she entered a dreamy state and then fell fast asleep.

CHAPTER 8

Mickey jolted awake when her head and shoulder slammed against the bulkhead and she was tossed out of her bunk onto the deck. The deck shook violently. She heard a loud ripping sound, as though wood was being splintered. Disoriented in the nearly pitch dark, she reached out, but grabbed only air as she rolled across the cabin deck. Her shoulder smashed into the closed cabin door.

At first she didn't know where she was. Then it all came back as the ripping sound subsided and she heard waves slapping against the hull. The deck was at a steep angle, which was not unusual when under sail. But the boat wasn't moving.

Trying to get her bearings, she looked up at the portholes. Out of the glass square in the overhead she saw stars. Out of the glass square in the bulkhead above the top bunk she also saw stars. It took a few moments for her mind to make sense of what she was seeing, and the extreme slant of the deck. The starboard side and bow were pitched up, and the boat wasn't moving forward.

As Mickey pulled herself up by the door handle and got to her feet, the boat began to slide to one side. She once again heard the loud ripping sound, which stopped as the boat flattened out and began to rock with the movement of the waves.

Mickey pulled a pair of jean shorts over her yoga shorts and flung the door open. She stepped into the passageway and then made her way through the saloon. A single light in the galley cast a dull glow throughout the interior. A couple of pots from the stove and some books littered the deck, but otherwise the saloon and galley were in order. She peered down the dark passageway next to the navigation station and wondered why Susan was not up. Mickey looked at the ladder and thought about going up to the cockpit first, but then decided to check on Susan.

Mickey moved quickly down the passageway to the aft cabin. She opened the door and found the room dark, except for a bit of light provided by the stars and a partial moon through the portholes. Susan's bed was empty, and Mickey figured she was up in the cockpit. As she turned to leave, Mickey caught sight of a dark blob lying on the deck, between the two beds. She continued into the room and knelt next to the blob. The blob was Susan's unconscious body.

Mickey bent lower and put her ear next to Susan's mouth and heard the gentle in and out of Susan breathing. Mickey stroked her hair and immediately felt the wet stickiness that had to be blood. Then she saw the dark gash above her right eye.

Mickey looked around the floor for something she could use to bind the wound and stop the bleeding. She grabbed one of Thomas' long-sleeve t-shirts lying on top of the bed. Mickey ripped off one of the sleeves and wrapped it around Susan's head. She secured the makeshift bandage with a knot.

Mickey checked to make sure Susan was still breathing before she stood and made her way out of the room and down the corridor. She turned and bounded up the ladder, wondering what Thomas was doing during all the mayhem.

She entered the cockpit and looked around. The cockpit was deserted; no Thomas. She then heard splashing and pounding against the outside of the starboard hull. She hurried over, peered over the guard rail, and saw Thomas floundering, hanging over the side, his head just below the surface. His lifeline was pulled tight as it stretched over the rail.

Mickey called out his name, grabbed hold of the line, and heaved.

Thomas' head broke the surface and he immediately spit out a mouth full of water before taking a deep breath. He, too, had a gash on his forehead, just below the hairline. Trickles of blood streamed down his face. He sluggishly reached up and grabbed hold of the lifeline with one hand while he coughed water from his lungs.

"Thomas! What happened?" Mickey screeched.

Thomas took a deep breath. "Must have hit something."

"A reef?"

"There are no reefs out here," he sputtered. "Something in the water. Something big. I was dozing at the helm. The next thing I know, you called my name. I must have blacked out."

"How do I get you back in the boat?"

Thomas tried to reach up for the railing with his other arm, but he was not able to raise himself high enough. "You'll have to release the lifeline so I can swim around to the transom."

Suddenly the boat pitched to the side. The lifeline lifted Thomas partially out of the water and bounced him against the hull. He floundered against the hull, but was not able to get hold of anything except the line.

"The sails are still up," he said. "Release the sheets and let the sails swing to neutral."

Mickey dashed to the helm, took a moment to study the lines, and then released the necessary clutched lines.

The main and jib swung to port, and the boat rolled back to an upright position.

Mickey ran back to the starboard gunwale and peered over the side at Thomas, with only his head above the surface. She ran her hand along the lifeline to where it hooked into the cockpit. She unscrewed the carabiner gate, pushed the gate in, and pulled on the strap to release the tension, but couldn't get enough slack to unhook the carabiner. She tried pulling on the strap with both hands, but it wouldn't budge. Thomas' weight on the other end was too much.

Mickey remembered the filet knives Thomas kept in a locker near the helm. She slammed the locker door open, retrieved a knife, and sliced through the strap. The end of the strap whipped itself toward the railing and came to a stop just before going over. Mickey grabbed the end and pulled while looking over the side. Thomas bobbed back to the surface and sputtered while trying to take a breath.

As Mickey worked the strap around to the transom, she realized the stern was higher out of the water than normal and the deck was angled down toward the bow. She turned and looked down the deck toward the bow, but could see nothing through the darkness. Based on the angle, she guessed the bow was taking on water.

She returned her attention to Thomas and worked faster to pull him around to the transom. Finally, he was far enough around that he could grab hold of the first step. Mickey helped as best she could as he struggled to pull himself out of the water.

After considerable effort, he had both elbows on the first step, and then a knee. He wiped blood from his eyes and then grabbed hold of the ladder.

"Where's Susan?" he gasped.

"She's still in the aft cabin, unconscious. She hit her head just like you did."

"I need to get her out of there," he said, as he struggled to get his foot on the first step. He then went up the three-step transom and stepped over the guardrail.

Back in the cockpit, Thomas used a rag to wipe more blood from his face. He looked at Mickey and then opened a locker. His hand came up with a life vest, which he shoved toward her. "Put this on."

"What about Susan?" Mickey asked as she took the vest.

"I'll get Susan, just put that on," he said, as he turned and wobbled off toward the hatch.

Mickey had trouble standing upright and realized the boat was at much more of an angle with the bow down.

She began to panic as she fought to remember how the life vest went on. She put the vest over her head and then pulled at the straps, trying to remember what went where. She managed to get one strap clipped in before anxiety took over and she abandoned the effort.

She wondered what was taking Thomas so long. She turned and made her way to the hatch, but before stepping on the ladder, she looked up toward the bow and thought of the compacted life raft secured to the deck just behind the mast. During her first tour of the deck, Thomas had pointed out the raft, how it was secured, and how to release it. But that was days ago.

She looked down the ladder into the darkness, and then back to the bow. If Susan was still unconscious, Thomas might need help to get her out. But if the boat went down, the life raft would be crucial to their survival. She opted for the raft, hoping Thomas could handle Susan.

Mickey bounded out of the cockpit, ran down the deck, and slid to a stop next to the raft. She peered into the night toward the bow. The star and moonlight reflected off the water, which was inching its way up the deck. She judged that the forward pulpit, the metal railing that extended beyond the bow, was already almost completely under water.

She bent to the raft and tried to remember how to release the square package. She ran her fingers round the edges and along the surfaces, feeling for the release clips. Her hands shook, and it took every bit of willpower to maintain focus and keep her anxiety under control. She glanced back at the advancing water line and then back to the raft. She thought of Thomas and Susan and where the water line might be inside the boat. It was obviously taking on a lot of water.

When the water reached her feet, she panicked. Her entire body trembled from fear and her mind raced. Torn, she didn't know whether to continue with the raft, or head back and help Thomas. She glanced toward the stern and saw no activity, which meant Thomas and Susan were still below. She looked at the raft, then at the water starting to rise over her ankle bone, and then toward the stern. She finally made up her mind and darted off toward the cockpit, leaving the raft still attached to the deck.

In the cockpit she slid up to the hatch and then bounded down the ladder. Her foot plunged into water as she stepped to the saloon's deck. The water covered her calf. She sensed that the forward area, her berth, and part of the saloon were already submerged.

Suddenly the boat rolled to starboard, and she heard the main boom slam to a stop against its sheet line.

Mickey reached for the galley countertop, took hold with one hand, but was unable to control her weight as she spun around and lost her footing. She splashed into the water and then felt the boat's deck dip toward the bow. She scrambled with feet and hands for purchase as she slid deeper into the saloon and the rising water. Mickey called out for Thomas and Susan as she struggled in the water.

She finally got a foot against the saloon table and then a hand-hold on the galley counter. When she heard water gurgling up from the bow she went into full panic mode. Her hands and lips trembled uncontrollably. Anxiety raced up her spine and settled at the base of her skull. Her neck and shoulders tensed. Her mind went blank.

She called out for Thomas and Susan again, but got no response. She looked at the dark passageway leading to the aft cabin. She tried to scramble in that direction, but with little to grab hold of and the steep angle of the deck canted to one side, she made little headway.

As the water line inched toward the ladder, Mickey began to float with the buoyancy of her life vest. She grabbed hold of the nav station bulkhead and tried to pull herself up into the passageway, but the deck was already at too much of an angle. She lost her grip and slid back into the rising water.

She called out for Thomas and Susan again and again as the water bubbled up the ladder and toward the hatch, forcing Mickey out the opening and into the cockpit. Her mind went into complete overload as she thought of Thomas and Susan still in the aft cabin, either trapped or unconscious.

Extreme anxiety and fear crawled up her back again. Her mind fogged as jumbled thoughts pinged back and forth. She lost all sense of focus as the rising water propelled her over the gunwale. She grabbed at sections of the guardrail as the boat began to slip below the surface.

Tears and seawater stung her eyes as she scrambled for handholds and screamed out for Thomas and Susan. The boat continued to slip past her grasps until she found herself bobbing, with nothing in her hands but water. The transom wobbled a few feet away as the white fiberglass hull inched its way below the surface in a turbulence of bubbles.

Tears streamed down her cheeks, and she screamed for Thomas and Susan until she realized that her voice was the only sound she heard. The boat was gone.

She used her arms to propel herself around as she looked in all directions into the night. She was alone with only the stars, the water, and the gentle breeze for company.

***

The only thing Mickey had in her favor at the moment was that she didn't sleep nude. The black sports top, white t-shirt, and black polyester stretch yoga shorts she wore to bed earlier in the evening, along with the jean shorts she managed to slip on, clung to her skin under the life vest. Her feet, legs, and arms were bare against the salty water.

Except for the stars and moon, all was dark as she floated alone in the middle of the largest ocean in the world. In a nearly catatonic state, she clutched the vest with both hands. Her chin rested against her chest, just above the water.

After what seemed like hours, she opened her eyes, afraid of what she might see, or not see. The ocean was a shade or two lighter and she figured sunrise was just over the horizon. She looked in all directions and saw only ripples and open sea. In the distance, she spotted something sticking just above the surface. A dark object. It would disappear beneath the waves and then bob back up. It just sat there and rolled back and forth with the motion of the waves. Disappearing, and then reappearing.

Since Mickey had to hold the vest with both hands to keep it from slipping over her head, she began kicking her feet to propel herself in the direction of the object. She had never been good at judging distances, but she thought the object was at least half a football field away, maybe more.

While she kicked, she used one hand to fumble with the life vest straps. She inhaled deeply and tried to think how the straps were supposed to go, and why she kept slipping out. She then remembered that two straps needed to go between her legs. She felt around and fingered each of the straps and their buckles. With one hand she fed a strap through her legs from behind and held it tight by squeezing her thighs together. She then reached around front, pulled the strap up, and snapped it into the appropriate buckle. She then found the second strap and went through the same process. With both straps buckled, she pulled each snug with one hand, and then hesitantly let go of the vest. It stayed in place. She then used both arms to increase her speed toward the object.

As she got closer, the object began to take shape. A dark reddish-brown and shaped like a pyramid, the point stuck out of the water about two feet when it was visible. It bobbed and rolled as the waves broke around it. With only a few feet between her and the object, she was able to see that one edge of the pyramid extended under water, down until it was out of sight. Then she saw that both of the other edges extended under water; the edge facing her extended almost straight down. The whole thing was massive, heavy, and barely buoyant.

She swam up to the object and placed a hand on the apex. Metal. Thick. She could just make out the first letter or two of some writing on the submerged side facing her. Then it popped into her mind. *A cargo container.*

Then she noticed a bit of white plastic streaked over the very tip of the apex. She slowly closed her eyes and dropped her chin. *This cargo container sunk the boat and killed my sister and brother-in-law.*

She felt intense anger come up from deep inside and then spill out into a loud, continuous scream. Tears returned as she relived the events from only a few hours earlier. After several screams, she began to get control of herself. She rested her chin on her chest and rested her hand on the apex of the cargo container. She remained in that position until the first rays of the sun warmed her face.

Mickey used both hands as she tried to climb up on the cargo container's corner. But with her weight, the container just rolled to one side, submerging her and her corner. Like a lumbering whale, her corner sunk and the corner on the other side popped up. When she let go, the mass slowly rolled back to its original position.

She tried several times to climb on top of the container. The large metal box just rolled with her weight. And with each maneuver, less and less of the metal body rolled back up to break the surface. Soon, nothing broke the surface, even when she left it untouched. Eventually, the large mass drifted lower, and lower, until it was out of sight. She wondered what it contained. Probably just more stuff from Asia, heading to eager Americans hungry for more.

Why didn't it sink before we came along, she thought. Anger returned, and then the tears, and then the despair.

CHAPTER 9

Mickey opened her eyes. Directly above, the sun beamed to earth with its warming rays as she bobbed in the chilly water.

She thought about how life could be all peace and tranquility one moment, and then turn to pure shit the next. It often took only seconds to shift from one to the other. Mickey had been through despair before, many times, in fact. She remembered being a happy child until her father left. When she got older, relationships started out with great promise only to turn south. Then she met Jack. He was everything she wanted in a man. She felt secure with him. He made her laugh. Moving in was exhilarating, the happiest she had ever been. Within six months she found out he was spending time with another. She threatened to move out. He apologized, said it would never happen again.

Life slowly returned to normal, and she thought maybe it was a one-time event. Then it happened again, and they went through recovery again. She wanted to move out, but she couldn't. She loved him; he loved her, he said. And then his latest escapade. Happiness to despair and back again. But all of that paled in comparison with her current situation. As she drifted, her mind replayed the events in her life and she wondered what she could have done differently.

Mickey jerked back to reality. She lifted her chin and blinked her eyes. Salt crusted her eyelashes. She swirled her arms to propel herself in a circle. Nothing but water in all directions. The sun blazed. She closed her eyes and rested her chin against her chest.

She thought back to the chart plotter and what she could remember about their last position. She remembered Thomas saying the currents and wind were in their favor for their westerly trek. *Not so much*, she thought, *for their southerly trek*. That meant she was probably moving west, maybe southwest, with the currents. She thought about Hawaii, probably a thousand miles in the wrong direction. Without fresh water she would be long dead from dehydration by the time her body washed up anywhere. And that would only be if her body survived the sharks.

Mickey stroked the surface and gently turned her body in a circle again. Water. There was nothing but water, in all directions. She felt her face with her wrinkled fingertips. She winced at the sharp sting of her sunburned face. It would only get worse. She licked her lips and tasted the salt crystals.

She thought about the sequence of events the night before and wondered if she could have done more, or something different. Dragging Susan to the cockpit, or even the saloon, might have made all the difference. But then Thomas would probably have drowned. She did not know why Thomas did not return to the cockpit with Susan in his arms. They must have gotten trapped. Or maybe Thomas passed out. She replayed different scenarios through her mind until her brain numbed from the effort. None of the scenarios turned out well.

She thought about the emergency position beacon installed on the boat. Thomas called it an Epirb. Even if it activated automatically, it probably wasn't sending much of a signal from under miles of ocean water. The chances of that signal being picked up were probably zero.

She thought about how long she would last floating in the middle of the Pacific, even if she wasn't gobbled up by a large fish. A person could go three weeks without food, but only three days without water. She wondered what toll the salt water would take on her skin the longer she remained submerged. She raised both hands out of the water and examined her wrinkled, prune like, fingers. How long before the layers began to separate? She didn't know, but probably not long. A matter of days, probably. Hopefully she'd be dead by then from dehydration.

Maybe Thomas and Susan were the lucky ones. They died quickly. They rested together, in their boat, on the ocean's bottom.

Mickey took in a deep breath and then exhaled slowly. She made another three-sixty degree scan of her surroundings. She glanced at the sun. With both hands she rubbed salt water on her sunburned face. It felt refreshing, but only for a few moments. The burning sensation returned quickly.

As the sun continued its journey to the horizon, the two nearly touching now, Mickey let her head rest back against the life vest. She swirled her hands gently in the water, careful not to move too quickly. Thrashing about would just attract unwanted visitors. The thought of seeing a fin in the water was beyond scary.

She thought about putting her head below the surface to check for predators. The thought of a large shark rising from the depths toward her was even more scary and sent shivers of fear through her body. She'd rather not know.

Then she realized the shivers were not from fear, but from the water feeling cooler as the sun sank lower. Only the top third hovered above the horizon. She shivered again and then folded her arms across her chest and grasped both shoulders. She lowered her chin to her chest and closed her eyes.

***

Two little girls, huddled together, hid in a dark closet. The smaller of the two fidgeted and giggled.

The older of the two shushed the younger. "Quiet, Mickey, he'll hear you," Susan whispered. "And stop moving."

Mickey put a finger to her lips and closed her eyes. She heard footsteps on the carpet outside the door. She opened her eyes wide and saw shadows under the door. The footsteps stopped for a moment and then moved away. Mickey giggled and then slapped her hand over her mouth.

Suddenly, the closet door flung open and light flooded in, illuminating the two girls.

A tall man stood in the doorway. "There you are," he boomed. He reached down and scooped up both girls in his arms, whisked them out of the closet, and onto the bed. The man began tickling them both. "This will teach you two, you can't hide from me."

Both girls giggled and laughed uncontrollably with contorted faces.

"You won't find me next time, Daddy," Mickey blurted between giggles.

***

Mickey blinked her eyes open and looked up at the stars twinkling in the night sky. She scanned her surroundings. Waves carried her up and then back down. They were larger than before, and the wind was stronger. She bobbed up and down, with nothing in sight except the stars above. She rested her head back against the life vest and gazed above. She tried to remember the constellations and find them in the sky. The big dipper was the only one she knew by name. At night she had no idea which direction was which, but she thought the big dipper was generally to the north.

She felt the water's coldness. Her cotton t-shirt offered no warmth. She went through bouts of uncontrollable shivering. Her teeth chattered. She licked her lips. They felt rough and chapped, crusted with salt. She was more thirsty than she thought possible. She thought about the long showers she used to take, back home, in Jack's house.

Jack? She wondered what Jack was doing and whether he had any concern for her and the dangers of an ocean voyage on a tiny sailboat. The more she thought about Jack, the more pissed she got. Really, this was all his fault. If it wasn't for his bullshit, she would not have agreed to go on the trip with Susan and Thomas. They might have left a day earlier, and would have missed the cargo container. They would be alive, continuing to live the life of a happy couple. It was Jack who snuffed out the lives of two people, Mickey's only family. Soon it would be three.

***

Mickey felt the wind in her hair, the sun on her face, and the boat under her feet as it bounced against the rolling waves. She held tight to the forestay and leaned out, like the girl in the Titanic movie. Spray from the cresting waves wet her face. She glanced back at the cockpit and saw Thomas and Susan wave and smile. Mickey waved to them and then turned back to the open ocean. She stood firm as the boat sliced through waves large and small. The deck rose and fell with each wave. She felt exhilaration and joy like never before. She wanted to feel this way the rest of her life. Just blissful adventure, free from the surly bounds of living a desk-bound life. She smiled at the dolphins keeping pace with the bow, just a few feet below where she stood. They were majestic, playful, living a life free from responsibility. Mickey made up her mind then and there that she would never go back. She would never return to the cold, gray, manmade canyons of New York City. This was where she belonged.

***

A wave slapped against the side of Mickey's face. Her head rolled to the side and then back. She felt herself bobbing, up and down. Water tickled the back of her neck. Afraid of what she might see, she kept her eyes shut. Another wave slapped her in the face. She blinked her eyes open, raised her head from its resting place against the life vest, and peered straight ahead. She hoped to see Thomas and Susan in the cockpit; Thomas behind the helm and Susan at the table. Both laughing.

Instead, Mickey saw only water. The sun suspended itself in the sky. And Mickey remembered the events that brought her to this time and place. Despair quickly replaced the joy she felt only moments earlier. Deep despair. She closed her eyes and tried to rejoin the dream. Another wave filled her ear with water. Sounds became muffled.

She opened her eyes and rolled her head to clear the water from her ear. Her hearing returned.

Tears welled up in her eyes as she thought about never seeing Thomas and Susan again. Her chin sunk to her chest and she closed her eyes. She willed for this to all be a bad dream and to wake up in her berth on the boat, or even back in New York. She slowly opened her eyes and saw water. Just water.

She licked her lips. Her tongue dislodged crystals of salt. She reached her hand up and rubbed her face. She felt salt crystals in her nostrils, eyebrows, and hair. She massaged her lips. Two spots stung from her touch. She fingered the spots and felt the cracks in her skin. She looked at her fingers. She looked closer at the bright white wrinkles that were once her fingertips. She rested her hands on her life vest and leaned back with her face skyward. She took in a deep breath and slowly exhaled. She swallowed. *Not much longer to wait.* She closed her eyes.

She felt the warmth of the sun subside, replaced with a cooler breeze. She opened her eyes to gray skies blocking the sun's rays. The wind had picked up, and the waves were higher, rolling with white crests. She heard a loud boom behind her, to the north. She used her arms to turn herself in that direction. From what she could see of the horizon, from the crest of the waves that carried her higher, it was all dark. Black, swirling, low-hanging clouds were fronted by sheets of gray. Rain. Heavy rain. She saw a flash and then almost immediately heard a loud boom, much louder than the one before. The wind became more intense, and the waves grew even higher. From the troughs she could see only high walls of water around her.

Soon, lightning flashed, thunder boomed, and torrents of rain pelted what little of her stuck out of the water. Mostly just her head. She turned her face up and opened her mouth. The rain drops stung as each smacked against her skin. She raised her hands and cupped them together at her mouth. Between crashing waves, she tried to pour what accumulated in her hands into her open mouth. She learned to judge the waves, closing her hands, mouth, and eyes as they broke, and then reopening to gather the fat rain drops. It worked. She tasted the fresh water and opened her mouth wider for more.

Strong winds and intermittent rains continued through the day and into the late afternoon. Mickey was able to gulp in the fresh water until she could drink no more. Then she just leaned back and rode the waves.

***

Vestiges of consciousness poked at her brain. She tried to will herself deeper, back into the sweet embrace of sleep. She pushed the rising tentacles of thought back down and made her mind focus on a dark empty void. But her mind refused to cooperate as her senses began to gather steam. Her first realization was that she wasn't moving. Maybe it all had been a dream and in reality she was snuggled deep in her covers. She moved a finger, hoping to feel the softness of her sheets. But all she felt was a swirl of water.

Reluctantly, and with great apprehension, she blinked her eyes open, hoping against all logic that she was snug in her bed at home. Water. As far as she could see, just water.

She used gentle hand strokes to turn her body in a full circle. She raised an eyebrow and turned another full circle as she stared out at a flat Pacific Ocean. With barely a ripple, and almost no wind, the sea stretched to the horizon in all directions.

The sinking sun shot the last of its rays against Mickey's face. It was warm in contrast to the cool water that covered everything below her neck.

She leaned her head back and rested against the life vest. She tried not to think of recent events, but her efforts were in vain. Images, like stills taken from a movie, flashed through her brain. One image in particular played over and over. It was the fear-etched face of Thomas when he glanced back at Mickey, just before he went through the hatch. It was as though he knew they would not see each other again. She tried to remember if he gave any kind of sign. Maybe there was a slight nod of his chin. Maybe not.

Mickey raised her head and flicked her hand to turn her body. She had no sensation of any current moving her, but then there was nothing from which to judge movement. She could be moving at ten knots, or perfectly stationary. There was no way to know.

Suddenly, the realization of hunger popped in her mind. She tried to count the days since she had eaten. Two days; no, it was three. She concentrated on the days and nights. This was still day two in the water. She thought about the storm, the harsh sun the day before, the boat's sinking the night before that, and the scrumptious dinner she enjoyed with Thomas and Susan at the end of their last day together.

She felt hungry, but knew she could go many more days without food. Water, on the other hand, was a problem. She already felt thirsty again, even after having drunk so much only hours earlier during the storm.

She looked upward. Not a cloud in the sky, horizon to horizon. Just blue. Blue sky and blue water.

She remembered what Susan had said. *The sun, the sky, the wind, the water, and us. Surrounded by the blue.* Funny how circumstances—a boat sinking and the loss of her sister and brother-in-law—could change the same sun, sky, wind, and water from euphoric, to pure misery.

CHAPTER 10

Groggy and disoriented, Mickey slowly raised her head and opened her eyes. She tried to focus, to think, but her mind remained in a fog. She raised a hand and felt her lips. They felt rough, swollen, and tender. Salt crystals had returned. She tried to look into the distance, but just keeping her eyes open took major effort.

She tried again to focus her mind. Slowly, she came more awake. She bobbed in moderate waves. In darkness. But there was light. The bright moon reflected off the water. She felt a breeze. How many days since the boat sank? She tried to count, but became lost in a fog. How long since she gulped in the fat raindrops from the storm? Her mind went blank, with intermittent flashes of confused thoughts and memories.

Then something took shape in the distance. Barely visible in the moon's dull glow. Slow, methodical, the shape appeared and then vanished, only to reappear. Dark, triangular. She worked to clear her mind, to understand what she was seeing. She blinked to narrowed her focus. She concentrated on the object as it moved through the water. A sense of fear rose up from the pit of her stomach before her mind finally grasped the object circling in the distance. Then her mind clicked. Shark.

Fear gripped her and anxiety ran up her spine. Without moving a muscle, she watched the beast circle, closing the gap. Bloody images of her body being torn to pieces flashed through her mind. Her fear doubled and then shot to a thousand times more than that. Her body shook, and she grew nauseous.

Just when she was thinking she had only one shark to contend with, another fin, farther in the distance, appeared and then vanished. A few yards beyond where it submerged, it appeared again. And then Mickey saw another fin, and then another.

She tightened her lips, let out a slow exhale through her nose, and reconciled her mind to the inevitable. Images of her body torn to shreds in the middle of red-stained water paraded through her mind. Soon it would be over. She knew there was zero chance of surviving in an ocean with no food, little water, and apex predators galore. At least it would be over soon. She closed her eyes and let her head drift back until her face was toward the sky. She had never been all that religious, but nonetheless, she found herself asking God to just make it quick. Stop with the suspense already, just get it over with. Let her join Susan and Thomas.

As she accepted what was about to happen, the fear evaporated, tension left her shoulders, and she fell into a calmness she had never experienced. It was like lying in her bed and being draped with the finest of silks before floating off to sleep.

As a final reminder of her predicament, the fins popped back into her mind. She saw the first one gliding effortlessly through the water with barely a flick of its tail. Then she saw the others moving up and down, up and down, as they covered much more distance, in a wide arc. They moved differently. She had seen it before, recently. She tried to remember back, back to where and when she had seen that movement. And then she remembered.

Mickey blinked her eyes open and found herself face to face with a large porpoise. The long nose, perpetual smile, and kind eyes all flashed in the moonlight. Suddenly, he flicked his tail which propelled his body up, out of the water, and then backwards. The splash broke the eerie silence, and then he was gone.

She focused on the shark, still circling thirty yards out. The porpoises came into view, more than Mickey could count. They surrounded the shark, gliding through the water in parallel, until the distance between Mickey and the parade of animals increased. Slowly, the porpoises escorted the beast away. Mickey watched as the group grew smaller and smaller, until they were just a speck on the dark ocean surface. And then, without warning, a porpoise, maybe the one from before, leaped out of the water only a few feet in front of where Mickey floated. The playful mammal stabbed the surface and disappeared. The ocean quickly returned to its calm, flat condition. Mickey propelled herself in a slow circle as she scanned in all directions. The shark was gone.

Mickey turned her face to the sky and closed her eyes. Her face contorted and tears streamed down her cheeks.

***

Darkness closed around her, bringing the chills. Mickey shivered. Folding her arms over her chest helped, if only in her imagination. In the distance, beyond the horizon, she saw flashes of lightning. She watched the light show for what seemed like hours, hoping the rain would come. It didn't, and soon the flashes were gone.

Nights were the worst. They were cold, dark, and the waves gave no warning before they struck. Even as exhausted as she was, she slept only until the next wave jolted her to consciousness.

In the dark, she rubbed her face. Her skin felt rough and painful. She imagined how burnt she must be. After two full days with her face exposed to the sun, wind, and salt water, her skin was probably peeling to the point of bleeding. She held her hand in front of her eyes and tried to focus, but there was only darkness, too much darkness to make out any details. She rubbed her nose and felt the skin peel under her fingers. The salt water stung. She tried to think of something else.

She wondered what Jack was doing. It was daylight in New York. He was working. Or, just as likely, he was screwing some other hapless soul. The image of seeing him nude on top of the blond popped back in her mind. A wave of anger washed over her, but quickly subsided. There was no point in dwelling on such thoughts. Her mind turned to her time on the boat with Thomas and Susan, and how a once in a lifetime trip came to such an abrupt end. Probably no sense in dwelling on that, either.

Mickey rested the back of her head on the life vest and stared at the stars as the motion of the water rocked her back and forth. She focused on one particular star and watched as it shimmered against the blackness of space.

She tried to take her mind off her parched throat by turning herself in a slow, three-sixty degree scan of the night sky. She imagined seeing a cruise ship headed straight for her. Actually, the tiniest of fishing boats would do. But neither was present in her reality. The vast open sea was deserted. No lights on the horizon. All she could see was water and darkness.

She closed her eyes and immediately felt the world start to spin. She opened her eyes and stared into the distance. She knew enough about dehydration to know that dizziness was one of the symptoms of the extreme variety. Headache was another symptom. She tried to remember back to when hers started. It was at least the day prior, maybe before that. She was at least on night three since she entered the water, with nothing to drink except the gulps during the storm. From everything she had heard and read, people only lasted three days without water.

She peered at the sky in all directions, hoping to see clouds. There were none. Only stars. She remembered reading somewhere that because of the curvature of the earth, it was only twelve miles to the horizon. And that was standing up. Her eyes were pretty much at sea level, which meant she was seeing less than that. Four miles, maybe. *That's nothing when you're floating in the middle of the Pacific*. She had no idea where she was in relation to where the boat went down, or the nearest land. From the chart plotter she remembered some islands about mid way between Hawaii and Samoa. But for all she knew, the current was taking her in the opposite direction.

The night wore on; the moon climbed higher, and Mickey grew thirstier, dizzier, and weaker. Her body felt completely drained of any energy, and she felt nauseous. The pounding headache didn't help.

She closed her eyes. She contemplated just unfastening her life vest and letting her body sink. Her mind went through the motions. One buckle and then the other, while she held on with one hand. She could hear the sound of the plastic snap as the two pieces separated. She could feel the tug of the vest release her weight. Only her hand on the vest kept her head above the surface. She imagined letting go, one finger at a time, and then slowly sliding from the vest. She could see the vest floating on the surface as she sank deeper and deeper. The clear water grew dimmer as she went deeper. Soon the vest was only a dot, and she knew she was beyond the point of no return. Outside of her own body, she could see herself sinking deeper. Her eyes were closed. She could feel her senses becoming muted. There was just an ocean of darkness, with no sensations. No pain. No memories. Like drifting off to sleep.

She blinked her eyes open, cupped a bit of water in her hand, and splashed her face. She used both hands to scoop water and let it pour over her head. She looked down at the buckles of her vest. She felt their plastic texture. She fingered the release mechanism.

She let her head plop forward into her hands. The stretch on her neck felt good. It reminded her that she was still among the living. She massaged her temples and twisted her head until she heard the bones in her neck crack. That felt good, too.

She raised her head and splashed her face. And then she scanned the entire horizon again as she floated, gently bobbing with the waves. Still nothing. She leaned her head back against the vest and closed her eyes. She could see herself, out of body again, but this time from far above. She floated higher and higher; her head and vest growing smaller and smaller until she was a single grain of red floating on a vast empty ocean of blue.

***

Rain drops woke her. She opened her eyes to her still dark surroundings. There was only a light breeze; the sea was calm. She looked up at the sky to get her bearings and saw only darkness. There must be a cloud up there. A few more rain drops and then they stopped, leaving barely enough wetness to wash away the salt. She wiped her face with both hands, which just moved the crusted salt crystals around. They stung against her sunburnt skin. Suddenly she was lost in a reverie of a long hot shower, shampoo and conditioner for her hair, and moisturizer for her skin. The kind of long showers she took at home, back in New York. Back at Jack's house. Jack. That asshole.

She rested the back of her head against the vest and peered at the dark sky above. She let her mind examine her current status. Almost no water in what would soon be three days. Her headache was worse than ever; the back of her head pounded. Just opening her eyes was painful. Her face was burnt, cracked, and swollen. Touching it sent stinging barbs to her brain. The rest of her body consisted of loose, deeply wrinkled skin, blanched almost pure white. She was coming up on three days with no water. That would be the end point. Her final destination. She wondered how long her lifeless body would continue to float on the ocean. She shuddered at the thought.

Mickey took a deep breath, gazed at the stars a few seconds longer, and then closed her eyes.

CHAPTER 11

Mickey opened her eyes and found herself face to face with a man—an older man, late fifties, maybe sixties, wild white hair, scruffy gray beard, deep blue eyes. Kind eyes. Mickey figured she must be dreaming or hallucinating, so she closed her eyes. Mickey heard a deep voice.

"I wasn't sure you were going to make it."

Must be auditory hallucinations, she thought. Mickey opened her eyes again. The man was still there, looking down at her. She blinked a couple of times and glanced down at her body. She was lying on a bed. "Where am I? And who are you?"

"My name is Travis Turner and you're on an island, actually an atoll. It's called Palmyra Atoll."

Mickey tried to sit up, but didn't have the energy, so she let her head plop back onto the pillow. She turned her head and peered at the bed she was on and the four walls around her. "How did I get here?"

"Before I go into a lot of explanation, sip some of this," Travis said, as he extended a cup toward her lips.

"What is it?"

"Coconut water. You're dehydrated to the point that drinking water may not bring you out of it. Your body is depleted of electrolytes. Coconut water is chock full of just what you need. Especially potassium. More than bananas."

Mickey raised her head and guided the cup to her lips. She sipped and then tried to gulp.

Travis pulled the cup back. "Just sip it, slowly."

Mickey guided the cup back to her lips and sipped.

After a few seconds Travis pulled the cup away. "That's enough to start. Let's see how you do, and then we'll try some more in a few minutes."

Mickey glanced at her body. She was still wearing the jean shorts over her yoga shorts and the white t-shirt over the black sports top, exactly what she wore the night she jumped from the boat. She licked her lips, took a deep breath, and let her head fall back to the pillow. Only her intense thirst and lack of energy filled her mind, but then her mind floated back to the past days—the boat sinking, with Thomas and Susan on board, floating upon the ocean for who knows how long, and now here, on this island. "How did I get here?"

Travis sat the cup on the rough-cut wood table beside the bed and sat back in his chair. "I found you floating in the surf this morning. I have no idea how you made it through the breakers and over the reef."

Mickey raised her hand and rubbed her face. It felt rough and tender.

"What's your name, and how did you come to be floating in the middle of the Pacific?"

Mickey licked her lips again. They were rough, with several spots that stung as her tongue passed over. She swallowed hard. "Michelle. Friends and family call me Mickey." She suddenly realized she had no family. Susan was the last of their clan. Mother and father died years ago. Mickey was without family. She closed her eyes for several seconds and then opened them to see Travis waiting patiently. "I was on a sailboat with my sister and brother-in-law. We hit a cargo container in the night. The boat went down with them still on board."

"Lucky you had the life vest on," Travis said, as he picked up the cup and extended it toward her mouth.

She raised her head and sipped the cool liquid until the cup was empty. She lowered her head to the pillow.

Travis stood with the cup and stepped across the room to a table. He refilled the cup from a pitcher. "You'll need to keep sipping this for the next few hours," he said, as he returned to her bedside and sat in the chair next to the bed. "If all goes well with that, we'll get some food in your stomach."

Mickey nodded as she raised her hand for the cup.

Travis handed her the cup and helped her guide it to her mouth.

She took several sips and then pushed the cup away. "What is this place, this building?"

"Research facility," Travis said, as he sat the cup on the table. "They study the marine animals and tropical island vegetation. This is one of the few, maybe the only, uninhabited islands with a rain forest."

Mickey turned her head. "Are there others here?"

"No. The researchers are here only a few months out of each year. They won't be back for several months."

"What about you?"

"I'm on my own. Came here on my boat."

Mickey opened her eyes wide. "If you have a boat, you must have a radio. Or this place must have a radio."

"Sorry, they take all the electronic equipment when they leave. And my boat only has VHF."

Mickey raised her head. "But you have a boat."

"We can talk about that when you're rested and get some of your strength back. Right now, you just need to keep sipping the coconut water and rest."

Mickey reached for the cup.

Travis picked it up and placed it in her hand.

She took a sip and then a bigger sip.

"Trust me, you'll want to take it real slow. If you drink it too fast, it will just come back up. Small sips every few minutes."

Mickey placed the cup on the table, rested back against the pillow, and tried to relax. Images of the boat sinking, Thomas and Susan, the open ocean, the shark, the blazing sun, and the shivering nights flashed through her mind. She tried focusing on her surroundings. The room was small, maybe ten by ten. There was a screen door to the outside. The walls, ceiling, and floor were wood. Bright sunlight flooded through the door and a screened window. The air was stuffy and hot.

"I'll let you rest a bit," Travis said, as he stood and moved toward the door. "I'll be back to check on you in an hour." He then disappeared through the door.

Mickey took more sips from the cup and then placed it on the table. She ran her hand over her t-shirt and shorts. They were dry, but wrinkled and stiff from embedded salt and sand.

Mickey tried to think of anything except the boat, Thomas, and Susan. She thought of Jack and work. She thought of Janet. No one would be wondering or worried about her not calling. Mickey told Janet the trip to Samoa would take ten or twelve days, maybe two weeks. She couldn't remember exactly. They were four or five days into their trip when the boat went down. She tried to count the number of days she drifted in the ocean. She had lost track, but probably not long enough for Janet or Jack to wonder.

She took more drinks from the cup, and then crossed her legs, closed her eyes, and tried to relax.

Mickey awoke at the sound of footsteps entering the room. She turned her head and saw Travis approaching with a stock of bananas in his hand.

"Let's try something easy on your stomach," Travis said, as he plucked a banana and removed the peeling. He placed the peeled fruit in Mickey's hand.

She took small bites, chewed, and swallowed until the banana was gone.

"How do you feel?" Travis asked, as he stood next to the bed.

"I feel better," Mickey said. She sat up slowly and swung her feet to the floor. She lifted the cup and took several sips of the coconut water.

"Can you stand?"

"I think so," Mickey said. She used her hands on the bed as support and then raised herself.

Travis took hold of an arm for added support.

Mickey wobbled a bit and then stood with both feet planted.

Travis helped her take a step, and then another. "Sit over here and eat another banana," he said, as he guided her to a wood straight-back chair next to a small rough-cut table.

Mickey took a seat and then took another banana from Travis's outstretched hand.

"Bananas didn't come naturally to the island," Travis said. "They were planted in the fifties and then replanted each time a hurricane washed salt water over the island, killing them. There hasn't been a major hurricane here in several years, so the bananas are back."

"Tell me about your boat," Mickey said, as she munched on the banana.

Travis took a deep breath, retrieved the cup of coconut water, and then took a seat in a chair on the opposite side of the table. He placed the cup and the stock of bananas on the table between them. "Sailboat, a cat," he said.

"When will you be leaving?" Mickey asked and then took several sips from the cup.

"I won't," Travis said, as he stared down at the table.

Mickey stopped drinking and locked onto his face as she slowly sat the cup on the table. "But— "

Travis looked up from the table. "Two reasons."

Mickey leaned forward.

"There's a very narrow cut through the reef into the lagoon," Travis said. "I motored in, but no longer have the fuel to motor out. I used it on the dinghy for fishing. Sailing out, or trying to swim the boat out, would be impossible."

"Why would you trap yourself on this island?"

"Reason two." He kept his eyes locked on Mickey's eyes. "I'm dying. I came here with no intention of leaving."

Mickey sat back in her chair and shook her head. "That's crazy. Why aren't you in a hospital, or at least near medical facilities?"

"I was. Lived in Honolulu until a month ago. They gave me six months, tops. Said there was nothing they could do to stop the cancer."

"What about chemo or radiation? I hear they have targeted drugs now that work wonders."

"None of that will work for me. And I prefer to live my last days here."

Mickey placed both hands on the table, palms flat, and raised her chin to the ceiling. She looked around the room and then back to Travis. "There must be a way for me to get off this island. I need to report the loss of my sister and the boat."

Travis pushed his bottom lip to one side with his index finger then rubbed the whiskers on his face. "At least you're not floating in the ocean, or at the bottom of it."

"Can I see your boat?"

"Sure," Travis said. "You can have the boat. In the morning. Tonight, just rest, and eat, and drink. There's fresh water for a shower in the next building over." He pointed in that direction. "I'll be in the galley, the mostly screened building next to the water, whipping something up for dinner." He looked at the watch on his arm. "There's soap and a towel in the shower building. Then rest. I'll see you about sundown." He stood, smiled at Mickey, and left.

Mickey heard the door close. She looked down at her t-shirt and shorts, both crusted with salt and sand. She felt her hair and found it in the same condition. She stood and walked over to the screen door.

She pushed the door open and stepped out into the bright sunlight. She saw several small buildings close by, and one larger building, probably the screened main building, in the distance. Beyond the larger building she could see light blue-green water. She walked to the shower building that Travis pointed out and stepped up on the wood platform that served as a small porch. Inside, she found showers and sinks, no toilets. On an island like this she figured the toilets were in a different building, separated from all the rest. The walls and fixtures inside the shower building were dated and had seen a lot of use, but were basically clean. She saw a towel hanging from a wooden peg stuck in the wall, and a bar of soap on the back of one of the sinks. She stepped to the sink and peered into a small mirror attached to the wall. She looked at her face in the reflection and then slowly closed her eyes. She waited for several seconds and then looked back into the mirror. She didn't recognize herself. Her blond hair was a matted mass of sand and salt. Her face, especially her nose, was crimson red and her cheeks were swollen, her eyes sunk into their sockets. Flaking skin covered her face and neck. She took a deep breath and turned away from the mirror.

She looked down at her clothes and then back at the door to the building. She felt wary of stripping down with a strange man only a few feet away. He might walk in as soon as he heard the water running. Mickey actually had a good feeling about him, but her character assessments of men had been proven wrong on numerous occasions, starting with her own father. Little did she know that he had cheated on her mother pretty much from day one. But Travis could easily take advantage of her if he wanted, at any time, especially in her weakened state. He seemed sincere. Mickey had no real choice but to trust him.

Mickey stripped off her t-shirt, sports top, and both pair of shorts, and dropped them all in a pile on the floor. She stood nude and examined the rest of her body. She was probably down ten pounds from her normal hundred and twenty. Her legs, feet, and arms were burnt, but not as bad as her face. Most of her skin below her neck was covered with a red rash and she saw several sores. In short, she was a mess.

She turned to the sink and twisted the water on. Only the cold water faucet worked. With the water running, she rinsed each article of clothing to get rid of the salt and sand, and then used the bar of soap to wash them. She rinsed again and then twisted as much water out as possible. Holding the wet ball of clothing, she looked around the room for a place to hang them. There was none, so she left them in the sink.

She took the bar of soap to the shower and turned on the water. She then stepped in and let the cold water rinse the grime away. She figured it was important to conserve the fresh water, so she turned the water off while she lathered her hair and body. She watched the sand-infused bubbles slide down her legs and accumulate around the drain. She flipped the water back on and rinsed.

She turned the water off, stepped from the shower, and toweled off. She glanced in the mirror again. There was improvement, but not much.

She wrapped herself in the towel, picked up the ball of wet clothes, and cautiously stepped to the door. She peered out to the neatly kept area, a courtyard of sorts. Travis was not around, and she didn't hear anything that would indicate anyone was in the area or approaching.

She spotted a few feet of cord stretched between two trees nearby. *Must be the clothes line*, she thought. With no one in sight, and her top and bottom wrapped in the towel, she stepped out of the door and inched toward the line while scanning in all directions.

Mickey swung each article of clothing over the line, spread them out so they would dry quicker, and then shuffled back to her cabin. She stepped over to the table and filled her cup with more coconut water from the pitcher. She sipped the liquid while she moved back to the screen door. She felt a breeze through the screen—warm air, but cooler than the air inside the room. There was no movement outside. She had no idea what time it was, but based on the sun, it had to be an hour or so past noon. She remembered that Travis said he would see her around sundown. She looked at the bed, finished the cup of coconut water, and placed the cup on the table. She stepped over to the bed, unwrapped the damp towel, and hung it over the back of the chair that Travis sat in. The sheet on top of the bed was a bit sandy from where she had reclined before. She flipped the sheet up and slid under.

She thought about where she had been, and how close she had been to death. Near death one minute;

taking a shower the next. She rolled to her side and closed her eyes.

CHAPTER 12

Mickey jolted awake when she heard the door open. She rolled to her back, pulled the sheet up to her neck, and watched Travis walk into the room.

He laid her dry clothes on the foot of her bed. "You look a little better," he said, as he immediately turned and started back for the door. "Dinner's ready." He then disappeared out the door.

Mickey eyed her clothes and then checked to make sure Travis was out of sight. She then pulled the sheet back, stood nude in the middle of the room, and reached for her clothes. She stepped into her jean shorts and then pulled her sports top and t-shirt over her head. She pulled the bottom of her t-shirt up and smelled. The shirt wasn't machine washed clean, but it was a thousand times better than it was. And despite having lost ten pounds, the shorts still fit snugly low on her waist. She left the yoga shorts on the bed.

She ran her fingers through her hair a few times and then padded barefoot across the floor and out the door.

The sun cast long shadows across the ground, and beams of light from her right filtered through the trees. She stepped off, across the sandy soil, toward the screened building on the water. From a single light inside, she could see Travis moving back and forth. She pulled the screen door open and stepped in just as Travis placed a pot on one of the tables. From the aroma she could tell it was boiled rice and roasted fish. "Smells wonderful," she said, as she approached the table.

"Sit," Travis said, as he motioned to one of the two plates. He then switched off the burner, moved a sizzling skillet to the table, and took a seat behind the second plate.

Mickey glanced at the two filets, and then at the stove.

"Propane gas stove, same as what I have on my boat," Travis said. "I figured fish and rice would be easy on your stomach."

"Thank you," Mickey said, "for this, and for pulling me out of the water." She smiled.

Travis smiled and nodded. "Least I could do. Dig in while it's hot."

Mickey used her fork to scoop some rice on her plate and half a filet.

Travis glanced at her place. "Take small bites and eat slowly." He slid a glass of water toward her. "Sip the water to wash it down."

Mickey separated a small piece of the fish with her fork, scooped it with some rice, placed it in her mouth, and chewed. She paused with the food still in her mouth and closed her eyes. She continued chewing and swallowed. "This is wonderful."

"Caught it this afternoon. Out past the reef, in my dinghy."

"I thought you didn't have gas for a boat?"

"I don't," he said. "I've been reduced to rowing in my old age. The gas was gone within two weeks after I arrived. I enjoy the rowing. Much quieter."

Mickey swallowed another bite. "I'm really sorry about your illness."

Travis exhaled. "Me, too."

"Do you have any family?" Mickey asked.

"A daughter, Clara," he replied. "About your age."

Mickey took another bite, chewed, and swallowed. "Does she know you are here?"

"No," he said, as he picked up his glass. He took a drink and then sat the glass down. "We lost touch years ago."

Mickey saw lines of regret etch across his face. She wanted to ask more, but since she had only just met the man, she decided against it. She just nodded. "Tell me about this place. Who built all the facilities?"

"The Navy occupied the atoll during the war, all four-point-five square miles. There're still remnants of the war scattered around. It's a US territory and Federal authorities have jurisdiction over anything that happens here."

"How often do people visit?"

Travis pushed his empty plate forward and leaned back in his chair.

"People cruising and fishermen can happen by anytime," Travis said. "Other than that, Federal officials visit occasionally. And there's the rotating mix of people from the Nature Conservancy and the Palmyra Atoll Research Consortium. Like I said, they study the marine life, the reef, and the vegetation on the islands. There are numerous islands, but this is the largest. The researchers built these facilities."

"And you don't expect anyone to happen by."

"It's always possible, but like I said, the researchers won't be back for several months."

"What about water?"

"There's no fresh water from the ground. But the facilities include a rain collection system. The water in the showers is gravity fed. There's also a generator for lights and pumps, but no fuel. The researchers bring the fuel when they come. So we have water, but no lights."

Mickey glanced at the flame in the lantern on the table and figured it, too, burned gas. She then placed her fork on the empty plate in front of her. "The dinner was a life saver, literally. Thank you."

Travis nodded as he stood and carried the plates and utensils to the sink. He began washing. "I'm sorry about your situation, but you're alive and the island provides enough resources to survive until someone shows."

Mickey squeezed her lips together as she stared at Travis's back. She nodded. "So what have you been doing since you arrived?"

"Fish, mostly. I try to keep the place tidy. And relax."

"Food?"

He turned around to face Mickey and leaned back against the counter. "I brought plenty of dry goods, rice, oatmeal, and such. I have some canned stuff left. The island provides fish, coconut, bananas, and papaya."

"Where do you sleep?"

"I kept to the boat for the first couple of weeks, but then decided the researchers wouldn't mind my using one of the cabins. I'm in the one next to yours."

Mickey looked back through the screen toward the cabins, but couldn't see anything through the pitch dark. "Are there any dangerous animals? Snakes?"

"No snakes," Travis said. "Nothing dangerous. But there are rats on the island, so it's best to close everything up at night. Otherwise, they'll come sniffing around."

"Through the screen door?"

"Nah, so far the screen has kept them out."

"Is there anything I can do before I turn in?" Mickey asked.

"Nope, you're good. Just get some rest. I'll show you the boat in the morning."

Mickey stood. "Thank you again. You saved my life."

Travis raised his chin slightly and lifted the corners of his mouth into half a smile. "I'll see you in the morning."

Mickey exited the main building and made her way to her cabin through the dark. Inside the cabin was even darker, and she had to feel her way to the bed. She sat on the edge, lifted her feet, and reclined back. She stared up into the darkness and thought about the day. She wondered how she was going to get back to Hawaii without waiting for someone to show up, either headed in that direction, or with a radio or satellite phone. There wasn't much she could do about it at the moment. Like Travis had said, at least she was alive.

***

Mickey woke to the sound of a bird's shrill squawking. She opened her eyes, but remained in bed while she listened to the bird, actually birds. It sounded like two of them. She listened to their calls as she wondered how long she would be on the island. She finally let out a long exhale and rolled to a standing position. She padded to the door and looked out at the courtyard. *Another day in paradise*. She saw Travis moving around in the main building. She looked at the top of a nearby tree and spotted the two birds in question. Both were brown with long beaks and a patch of white on their heads that gave the appearance of a flattop.

She pushed the door open and walked across the sand to the main building. "Good morning," she called out, as she opened the door and stepped in.

Travis turned to her and smiled. "How did you sleep?"

"I don't remember waking up in the night. I must have been really tired."

"No doubt," Travis said, as he turned back to the stove. "Feel like oatmeal and some coffee?"

"Anything is fine," Mickey said, as she took a seat.

Travis spooned the oatmeal from a pot into bowls and then added diced banana and papaya. He brought the two steaming bowls to the table and placed one in front of Mickey. "Is black coffee okay?"

"Black is fine," Mickey said. "The oatmeal looks wonderful."

"Sorry, no honey or sugar," Travis said, "but it's good for you. And easy to digest."

Mickey picked up her spoon and stirred the oats and fruit together. She lifted a scoop to her lips, blew on it a few seconds, and placed it in her mouth. She chewed slowly and then swallowed. "I didn't know oatmeal could taste so good."

"My specialty," Travis said. "I make it most mornings."

"I'm sorry you're going to all this trouble for me," Mickey said. "Let me know what I can do to help out."

"And extra mouth is no bother. I'd be doing the same if I were alone."

As they ate their breakfast, they chatted about the island. Travis talked about the many varieties of birds and the fish. He also talked about the many sharks he had seen outside the reef.

"Has anyone showed up while you've been here?" Mickey asked.

"Not a soul, except for you of course. Just as well. You never know what you might get with people. There are all kinds."

Mickey thought of Jack. "That's for sure."

They finished breakfast, washed and put away the dishes, and then Mickey followed Travis out the door and to the water's edge.

Mickey scanned the lagoon and then fixated on Travis's boat, anchored fifty yards out. "You sailed from Hawaii in that."

"Yep."

"It's small."

"Small, but capable," Travis said. "She's a Seawind 950 cat, about thirty feet. She got me here just fine. She's named Wispy, but I just call her cat."

Mickey stepped closer to the water. "Can we go on board?"

"This way," Travis said, as he started off toward a rubber dinghy tied to a palm tree.

Mickey followed Travis to the dinghy, watched as he untied the rope, and then stepped inside when he motioned.

He pushed off, then jumped aboard, and sat on the middle seat. He took hold of a pair of oars, backed the boat out, and then spun her around to face the catamaran. He rowed to the boat and pulled up at the starboard sugar scoop. He motioned for Mickey to climb aboard. "After you, young lady."

Mickey took the dinghy's line in hand and then stepped onto the cat. She climbed the three stairs to the deck and tied off.

Travis stepped up to the deck and into the cockpit. He opened his arms wide and raised a chin. "Well?"

"Like I said, she's small compared to the boat I was on."

"Let me show you around," Travis said, as he turned toward the bow and put his hand on the navigation pod. "Helm." He pointed to the instruments. "Chart plotter and AIS."

Mickey nodded as she stepped closer and perused the instruments. "Engine?"

Travis turned to his left and opened a locker. He then stepped to the other side of the cockpit and opened an opposite locker.

Mickey looked inside each locker and then at Travis. "Outboard motors?"

"Yep." He put his hand on a set of switches. "Electric to lower and raise, key ignition, and throttles." He pointed to the two throttles on the left side of the helm. He then turned and pointed at the solar panels mounted on the aft arch. "Solar charges the batteries when the engines are off."

"Does she have a water maker?"

"No, but the hardtop over the cockpit is guttered to collect rain water. Plus there's a sixty-six gallon tank on board, along with a forty gallon tank for fuel."

"Which is currently empty," Mickey said.

Travis nodded. "She has an autopilot, of course. Can't solo sail without one. She has a two foot seven inch draft, which is good, but not good enough for these reefs, except through the cut." He pointed toward the open ocean.

Mickey turned and saw a narrow channel of dark water leading through the reef. She then looked from one side of the boat to the other and then back at the channel. "It's barely wide enough for the boat."

"It's a little wider than it looks from here, but way too narrow to sail through, or even pull her through. You'd have the boat on the reef in a matter of seconds. Tear a hole in one or both hulls and you're done sailing."

Mickey looked around the cockpit, at the two engines, and the helm. She twisted her lips to one side, closed her eyes, and inhaled a deep breath.

"She's fast," Travis said. "I've had her up to almost twenty knots. Of course, it took a thirty knot breeze to do it."

Mickey walked over and took a seat at the cockpit table and sat back against the cushion.

"The table lowers to form an extra bunk if needed," Travis said, as he took a seat opposite her at the table. "You say you were on a monohull."

"Uh-huh," Mickey uttered, as she nodded.

"Sailing a cat is mostly the same, but with this one there's one important difference. Because she doesn't have a back stay, you have to be careful downwind. There's less support for the tension against the mast." He pointed to the port and starboard shroud lines. "The shrouds are positioned a little aft of center, which helps, but in a heavy downwind the forestay up front may slack."

"Good to know," Mickey said, as she stood. "Let's see the rest."

Travis led Mickey down the port ladder, turned aft, and opened a solid door. "One of two heads." He stepped inside, followed by Mickey.

Mickey stared at the toilet. "Pump toilet."

"Yep, works fine. Same on the starboard." He then squeezed past Mickey and led her down the passageway. He put his hand on a middle bunk as he passed. "Pass-through bunk, and there's a double bed cabin at the bow." He opened the forward cabin and let Mickey look around. He then motioned for Mickey to follow. He led her back up the ladder, across the cockpit, and down the starboard ladder into the galley. "Propane stove, icebox, fresh water faucet. And there's adequate storage." He pointed forward. "Another double bunk cabin in the bow, and the second head in the stern."

Mickey looked from aft to stern and then stepped back up the ladder to the cockpit.

Travis stepped up behind her. "Do you have any experience at sailing?"

"Just what I learned on the boat—before it sank."

"I'm guessing you had electric winches and furling main and jib."

Mickey nodded as she looked around for the winches.

"Halyards and sheets feed back to the cockpit. Hand winches. Furling jib, but it's a stacked main, which means you raise and lower the sail. Reef the sail in heavy winds. There's two reef points. I can show you."

Mickey turned and stared into Travis's eyes. "You sound like you're trying to sell me the boat."

"I am, of sorts." He took a seat at the cockpit table. "I'm not leaving this island. I'm happy knowing the boat will be put to good use. Or would be, if you could get a couple of gallons of gas."

Mickey took a seat at the table. "Yeah, looks like I'm not going anywhere without that."

CHAPTER 13

"You should probably stay out of the sun for a while," Travis said, as he stepped in the dinghy with a rod and reel, sat, and picked up the oars. "Relax in the shade and drink some water. Hopefully, I'll be back with dinner." He smiled and then began rowing.

Mickey watched as he rowed past the catamaran, through the channel, and just beyond the reef. He threw over a small anchor and then began fiddling with the rod and reel.

She walked back to the main building, poured herself a glass of water, and took a seat. She watched Travis in the distance, wearing his wide brim hat, toss the lure out and then reel it back in.

She thought about his situation and his intent to die on the island. She thought about Susan and Thomas, and at what point they knew they were going to die. Maybe they never did come to that realization. They might have both been unconscious at the time. She thought again about whether there was anything more she could have done; should have done. She remembered trying to make her way into the aft passageway and then being launched out of the hatch by the rising water. She remembered the water pushing her over the railing, and then watching the boat sink before her eyes. She tried, but did she try hard enough?

She replayed the scenario over and over in her mind and came to the conclusion that she should have tried harder. She could have gone to the aft cabin rather than the life raft. What good is a raft if you're dead? She could chalk it up to confusion, indecision, and fear. Mostly fear. At her young age, she already had regrets. Staying with Jack after he cheated the first time was a regret. There were others. But none compared to the regret she now felt about her lack of action on the boat. She knew it would be something she carried with her the rest of her life. The least she could do was report the loss to the authorities as soon as possible.

She ran her fingers through her hair and looked back out at Travis.

He was still tossing the lure out, with apparently no luck.

Mickey finished her glass of water and then walked back to her cabin where she looked at herself in the mirror. She couldn't tell if the sunburn on her face was better or worse. It was still red, and some spots were still peeling. The skin under the peeling was a bright pink. Travis was right; she should stay out of the sun as much as possible. At least she was getting her energy back. She felt like she would be able to help Travis more in a day or two. She could cook. And she could help with the fishing. Helping out would hopefully lessen the guilt she felt about eating his food. She certainly had no way to pay him. She had nothing except the clothes on her back. A single top, shirt, and two pair of shorts. That's all she had.

She looked down at her clothes. The shorts were okay, but the t-shirt already had a hole under the armpit. And speaking of armpits, she hadn't shaved those or her legs since at least two days before the boat sank. She would just have to deal with it. She certainly wasn't going to ask Travis for his razor. Given the shape of his beard, he probably didn't own a razor.

She shook her head in the mirror and felt stupid that she worried about such things. There was much more to think about. Her sister and brother-in-law had just died! And she needed to find a way off this island.

Mickey left the cabin and walked past the main building, to the water's edge. She saw Travis struggling with something on the end of his line. A fish, she presumed. A big one. With the dinghy held in place by the anchor, he dipped the pole, reeled, and then pulled the pole up. He did this over and over. Even from this distance Mickey could tell that Travis was tiring quickly. Each upswing seemed to take more out of him than the one before. She didn't know if it was his age or his illness. Probably both.

She watched as he continued to struggle. Pulling the fish the last few yards to the boat seemed to take every bit of energy he had. She felt sorry for his situation, but once again, there was nothing much she could do except stand there and watch.

***

Sweat streamed down Travis's face as he stepped from the dinghy holding an eighteen-inch tuna. He smiled as he raised the fish to show Mickey.

Mickey smiled back, despite the pain she saw on the man's face. She went forward and took the fish from his hand. "Are you alright?"

"Just a bit tired," Travis said, as he took a step in the sand. His knee went limp, and he dipped a bit before catching himself. "I probably just need to rest some."

Mickey placed the fish on the grass, well away from the water, and helped Travis the few steps to the shade of some palm trees, and then to a seat on the trunk of one of the trees. "Stay here. I'll get you some water."

He took in deep breaths and wiped his face with the sleeve of his shirt.

Mickey picked up the fish and hurried to the main building. She put the fish in the sink, poured a glass of water, and carried it back to Travis.

He accepted the glass with a nod and took a long drink. "I just need to sit here a bit. I'll be fine."

"You should take a break from fishing for a day or two," Mickey said, as she took a seat on the trunk next to him.

"One of the few joys left," he said. "I plan to fish until I can't."

"Well, at least let me go out with you tomorrow. I can help."

Travis stared at her face for several long seconds. "You need to stay out of the sun."

"I'll be fine. I saw another wide-brimmed hat on your boat. I can wear that."

Travis let out an exhale and then took another drink of water. "We'll see."

"Maybe we should go out in the morning, when it's cooler."

Travis nodded his head and then closed his eyes. He was obviously feeling the light breeze off the lagoon.

"If you'll be okay here, I'll go clean that fish," she said, as she stood.

"I'm okay," Travis said. "And there's rice and a can of beans."

"I'll take care of it," Mickey said, as she started off. "You just rest."

Two hours later, Mickey and Travis sat at a table in the main building with plates of food before them. Rather than the beans, Mickey opted to shred some coconut into the rice and top it with papaya. The fish, baked in the oven, turned out perfect. Nice and flakey. They ate as they talked.

Travis went into more detail about his boat and the differences between it and sailing a large monohull. He explained that he once owned a monohull, nearly fifty foot. He talked about cruising the islands. Days of boredom, separated by moments of sheer terror, he said. But overall he loved it. He loved every aspect of sailing, including the maintenance. And there was plenty of that. Something was always breaking. He talked about the people he met; island people and fellow cruisers. It was a community. He got to know several well enough to call them friends.

As Mickey munched and listened to his stories, she noted the light in his eyes and the excitement in his voice. She began to understand why he would want to spend his last days on an island.

"Why did you pick this island?" Mickey asked.

"I had stopped here several times during my trips around the Pacific. I got to know the researchers; they got to know me. Unlike most atolls, this island has resources. And I knew it was deserted for most of the year. The lagoon provides good cover from the weather. And the Navy was nice enough to cut the channel through the reef."

"How far is Hawaii?"

"A thousand miles due north. We're a little less than half way between Hawaii and Samoa."

"We were headed for Samoa when the boat sank," Mickey said.

Travis nodded. "What are the chances of running into a cargo container in this giant ocean?"

"Probably less than getting hit by an asteroid."

"Probably," Travis said.

"A thousand miles in a sailboat not meant to venture very far from a coast," Mickey said, as she shook her head.

"I did it."

"I'm not you," Mickey said. "I don't have your experience."

"Maybe you won't have to; maybe someone will come by headed for civilization."

"Maybe," Mickey said, as she stood, gathered the dishes, and carried them to the sink.

Travis went to stand up.

"Sit," Mickey said. "I'll take care of this."

Travis sat back down, lifted his glass, and took a drink. "Wish we had some beer."

"I'm surprised you don't."

"I did. Drank it all the first couple of weeks."

Mickey ran some water, washed the dishes, and put them away. "I think I'll grab a shower before I turn in."

Travis turned his attention to the blue water of the lagoon and the fading light of the sun. "I'll sit here for a while."

Mickey paid a visit to the toilets and then the shower. She followed the same routine as before: washed her clothes in the sink, showered, and then wrapped up with the towel. She draped her wet clothes over the makeshift clothes line and then tucked herself under the sheets just as the last of the sunlight faded to darkness.

***

With Mickey sitting in the front of the dinghy, Travis rowed to the catamaran.

Mickey tied up at the starboard sugar scoop and then hopped aboard. She made her way down the port ladder to the pass-through bunk. She found the extra hat on top. She grabbed the hat and then returned to the dinghy.

"Drape your t-shirt over your head and down the side of your face," Travis said. "And then put the hat on over that. The t-shirt will help protect your face from the sun."

Mickey pulled the t-shirt over her head, draped it as Travis suggested, and then put the hat on top. "Fits pretty well this way." She untied the line and pushed away from the catamaran.

Travis used the oars to spin the dinghy around until it faced the channel and the open sea. He rowed.

Mickey, wearing her black sports top and the hat and t-shirt contraption, felt ridiculous, but it worked. She picked up the rod and reel, fumbled with the mechanisms, and then turned the handle a couple of cranks. She watched the lure as it pulled to the tip of the rod. "What kind of lure is that?"

"It's a squid-looking gizmo. Works pretty good. I have several. This is for small-to-medium fish. And the rod and reel you're holding is a Penn Senator 113. The made-in-the-USA, newer version."

Mickey nodded as she sat the rod and reel down. "I don't mind rowing."

"On the way back. Have you fished before?"

"It's been a long time. Went with my dad when I was really young."

Travis rowed through the channel until they were just beyond the reef. He stopped and immediately threw the anchor overboard. He then picked up the rod and reel. "Let me show you how this works," he said, as he handled the reel. "Just pull this back." He pulled the gear lever back, held the spool with his thumb, swung the rod back over his right shoulder, and flung the lure out about twenty yards into the ocean. "Like so." He reengaged the gear and began winding the handle. "And then just reel it back in slowly. You can turn the clicker off if you want." He pointed to a switch on the side. When the lure was back to the tip of the rod, he handed it to Mickey.

Mickey followed what she saw Travis do, flicked the rod, and watched the lure plop into the water, four feet from the dinghy. She began winding.

"Timing is everything," Travis said. "Try it again, but concentrate on where the tip of the rod is when you release the spool."

Mickey swung the rod again and watched the lure hit the water ten yards out.

"A little more oomph with the arm and wrist. And more arc."

With each toss Mickey got better with the distance. After twenty minutes of sitting quietly, with Mickey tossing the lure over and over, there had been no bites.

"Just keep it up, reel a little slower, and enjoy the blue sky and the water."

Mickey smiled as she tossed the lure again.

They sat quietly for another ten minutes when Travis lifted his hat, scratched his head, and replaced it lower on his forehead. They both fixed on the lure running through the water.

"I left my family when Clara was only ten," Travis said.

Mickey glanced at Travis, but then looked back toward the lure without commenting.

"I felt like they were holding me back from my next adventure. I worked for some of the largest oil companies; traveled the world in search of their next oil field." Travis paused as he gazed at the open ocean. "I went back and forth with the idea of leaving for a couple of years, and finally just told my wife I couldn't do it any longer. I left." Travis waited a couple of beats. "In a way, I regretted it, but in a way I didn't. I regret it more now."

Mickey remained quiet, focused on her fishing.

"I've come to realize that what's most important in this life is the people who accompany you along the way. But I learned that way too late."

Mickey finally looked over at Travis. "My father did the same thing."

Travis raised his chin and snorted through his nose.

Mickey continued. "To this day I'm not sure why. Maybe it was for the same reason you did. Adventure.

Freedom. I think deep down inside, I've always felt I was somehow the cause."

"Honey, I haven't known you for very long," Travis said, "but one thing I know with absolute certainty, it wasn't your fault."

Mickey remained quiet.

"I have plenty of regrets, but one of the biggest is never saying those words to my own daughter. Somehow I just always thought she knew."

"Where are they now?"

"Wife, ex-wife, died about ten years ago. Her heart. Clara lives outside Orlando. Married. She's a Stevens now. Has two kids of her own."

"You talk to her then," Mickey said.

Travis rubbed his chin and then shook his head. "Not directly. I hired a PI a couple of years ago."

"Why haven't you gone to see her?" Mickey asked.

"Didn't want to disrupt her life after all these years. And I guess I didn't want her to feel sorry for me."

"It's not too late."

Travis looked toward the open sea without replying.

At that moment Mickey felt a tug on the line and whipped her head around to where she last saw the lure. She saw a swirl in the water and then felt a stronger tug. "I think I've got one."

Travis leaned toward her. "Pull up on the rod to set the hook."

Mickey pulled up, released the tension, and started reeling. Over and over, she pulled up against the weight of the fish, let the rod dip, and then reeled. The muscles in her arms and legs flexed with each upstroke. Pull and reel, pull and reel. "Feels like I hooked a whale," Mickey shouted.

"Just keep doing what you're doing," Travis said, as he scooted closer. "Bring him right up to the boat." He picked up a hand net from the bottom of the boat and got on his knees next to Mickey. "Keep reeling, you've almost got him here."

Mickey watched as the fish continued to fight. Her arms were becoming fatigued, and she breathed heavily. Drops of sweat slid down her forehead, through her brow, and into her eyes. She blinked to clear her vision, unable to take either hand off the rod. Soon she saw a flash of green, about ten yards from the boat.

"Looks like a nice-sized Mahi," Travis said. "Keep him coming."

Mickey lowered the rod, turned the handle, and pulled. Her energy was spent and her arms ached, but she kept it up. Finally, the fish gave up just as he came up to the side of the dinghy.

"Keep tension on the line," Travis said, as he scooped the fish into the net. He lifted the net and the fish into the air. "As big as the tuna yesterday."

Mickey let go of the tension. Still holding onto the rod, she let her arms rest on her legs. She dropped her head and took in several deep breaths. She then used one hand to wipe the sweat from her face with the t-shirt.

Travis lifted the fish into the boat and dropped him and the net in the bottom. He put one foot on the fish while he removed the hook from its mouth. "She's a nice one," he said, looking up at Mickey with a big smile.

Mickey smiled back and then wiped more sweat from her face. "And you do this every day?"

"As much as I can, weather permitting," Travis said, with the smile still stretched across his lips. "I think you said something about rowing back."

Mickey looked up into his eyes, blinked, and let out a long exhale. She nodded as she stood and shifted back to the rowing seat. She plopped down and then massaged her biceps and forearms. It did little to relieve the fatigue she felt in those muscles. Nonetheless, she grabbed both oars and rowed.

***

For the next five weeks Mickey and Travis fell into a routine that included fishing most mornings, when the weather permitted, lunch, free time, dinner, and then to bed at nightfall. During this time Mickey's lips returned to normal and her skin healed and turned a light brown, contrasting nicely against her blond hair.

Mickey had plenty of time to walk the island and swim. She used a swim mask and snorkel from Travis's boat to explore the lagoon. There were fins, as well, but they were too big. She supplemented their usual diet of fish with an occasional lobster.

She also decided to scrape the bottom of the catamaran's hulls to remove the growth that had accumulated since Travis first started out on his last journey. The work was hard, but she kept at it with the plastic scraper and a brush until the bottoms were smooth.

With Travis's help, she practiced raising, trimming, and lowering the sails. And she became familiar with the various lines, sheets, and halyards as she cranked them around the winches. Since the boat's batteries were always fully charged from the solar panels, Mickey familiarized herself with the autopilot, chart plotter, AIS, and the radio. After these sessions, when Travis returned to the facilities on shore, she took the opportunity to clean the boat of dirt and mold, and organize its provisions. She did a little each time she was on board until finally the boat was as clean, neat, and tidy as possible. The white bridge deck shined once again.

Between the diet of mostly fish and fruit, the exercise, and the restful sleep each night, Mickey gained back the ten pounds she lost, except it was all muscle this time. The muscles in her arms, legs, and abdomen became more and more defined. Physically, she felt the strongest she had ever felt.

Travis, on the other hand, grew weaker. His slim, wiry, frame became thinner. Just sitting in the dinghy while Mickey fished and rowed seemed to tire him more each day. Even though he looked exhausted most of the time, and he obviously was in some degree of pain, he never complained. He helped as much as possible, but by the end of the fifth week, Mickey was taking care of everything.

More and more, Mickey wondered how Travis would be able to cope when the pain got to be too much. And she wondered how she would be able to cope with watching him suffer. That's usually what she thought about each night before she drifted off to sleep.

But then, everything changed on the fortieth morning.

CHAPTER 14

Mickey blinked her eyes open and stared through the screen door at the dull light of dawn. Normally she slept a little longer, and got up when the sky was lighter. She closed her eyes in an attempt to doze a few more minutes. That's when she heard the barely audible, low-pitched whine of motors fading in and out.

She opened her eyes wide and listened, trying to determine if what she heard was real, or part of a dream. She heard it again, a little louder. Boat motors. In the lagoon.

Her torso shot up from the bed and she swung her feet to the floor. She stripped off her t-shirt and replaced it with her black sports top. Then she stood, slipped on her jean shorts, and moved to the door. She listened. It was definitely a boat she heard, and it was getting closer.

She pushed the screen door open and stepped outside just as Travis emerged from the adjacent cabin.

"A boat," Mickey said.

"Sounds like it," Travis said, as he stepped off in the direction of the lagoon.

Mickey fell in behind and they both marched to the water's edge.

Mickey's gaze fell on a cabin cruiser, a fishing boat, idling through the channel. She saw two men: one behind the wheel and one at the bow. The one at the bow kept his eyes peeled on the reef at each side of the boat.

Travis and Mickey looked at each other, and then back to the fishing boat.

When the boat cleared the end of the channel, the man on the bow stood up and looked toward Mickey and Travis standing on the beach. He then walked back and joined the other man in the cabin. The boat ambled along, engines bubbling, until it was fifty yards offshore. The anchor dropped, the engines quit, and all became quiet once again.

The two men shuffled from the cabin to the open stern and then hopped into a small rubber dinghy that had trailed the cruiser at the end of a line. One of the men grabbed a set of oars, while the other untied. The one man rowed with his back to the shore while the other man sat in the front. His eyes never left Travis and Mickey.

When the dinghy reached shallow water, a few yards from shore and a few yards down from where Travis and Mickey stood, the man sitting in the bow hopped out, grabbed a line, and pulled the dinghy up on the beach.

He had shoulder-length blond hair, straggly, a short beard, and was of medium height. Athletic build. He wore cut-off jeans, a t-shirt, and sandals. Mickey thought he was thirty-five or so. The other man was older, larger, fatter, Hispanic, also with straggly hair, dark. His eyes were dark, too. He seemed to have a perpetual grin. He wore a ragged Hawaiian shirt, red flowers, and khaki shorts. Barefooted. He also wore a large hunting knife belted to his hip. The younger man tied the dinghy to a palm tree and then approached, with the older man close behind.

"I'm Darrel," he said, as he jabbed his thumb over his shoulder. "This is Raphael."

Raphael raised his hand in a slight wave, but didn't say anything.

Travis took Darrel's hand and glanced at Raphael who remained several feet behind Darrel. "Nice to meet you. I'm Travis and this is Mickey."

Darrel turned his attention to Mickey and stuck out his hand. "Darrel."

Mickey shook his hand and then looked over his shoulder at the fishing boat. "Fishing this far from civilization."

Darrel glanced back at the boat. "Just cruising at the moment. Stopped by to replenish our fresh water."

Travis motioned as he turned toward the main building. "Come on up. I'll make some coffee." He led Mickey and the two men to the main building. Raphael brought up the rear, still smiling, but so far with nothing to say.

The two men took a seat at one of the tables while Mickey joined Travis at the stove.

She peered at Travis with a clenched jaw while he poured water into the coffee pot and set it on the stove.

Travis glanced at Mickey, tightened his lips, and raised his chin slightly.

Mickey didn't know if that was good or bad, but she turned to the two men and smiled. "Just cruising, from Hawaii?"

Darrel smiled as he locked eyes with Mickey. "Well, we've been all over, including Hawaii."

Raphael looked Mickey up and down and then settled on Mickey's face. "All over," he said, with a thick accent.

Darrel elbowed Raphael in the shoulder. "Excuse my friend here; we've been out awhile. You understand."

"Sure, I understand," she said, as she eyed Raphael. She then turned her eyes back to Darrel. "Where are you headed?"

Darrel paused while he raised his chin and rubbed along his beard's bottom edge. "Not sure. We play it by ear day to day." He lowered his chin and smoothed his mustache. "How long have you been here?"

"Couple of months for me," Travis said, as he turned from the counter to face the men.

"You both came here on the cat?" Darrel asked.

Travis looked at Mickey. "She's the victim of a mishap at sea. Boat sank, taking her sister and brother-in-law. She washed up on shore a few weeks ago."

"I need to get to Hawaii to report the loss," Mickey said. Her focus tightened on Darrel. "Unless you have a radio on your boat."

"I have a radio, but it won't reach Hawaii. Not even close."

"The coffee will be ready in a few minutes," Travis said, as he took a seat at the table.

Mickey remained standing.

"The only fresh water here is what we catch from the rain," Travis said. "The research facility here has a system. There's plenty for your boat."

"Thank you," Darrel said. "We have a few repairs to make on the boat. Maybe we can get to the water tomorrow."

"Yeah, tomorrow," Raphael grunted.

"That's fine," Travis said. "Whenever."

Travis turned to check on the percolator and then stood and moved to the stove. He took three cups from a cupboard and set them on the counter. He took his seat again. "How long you been out?" he asked.

Darrell glanced at Raphael and then rubbed his beard again. "A couple of weeks, I guess. Easy to lose count."

"Does your cat burn diesel?" Raphael asked.

"No, gasoline," Travis said. "Petrol."

Raphael gave a weak smile and nodded.

"Have you been to Palmyra before?" Travis asked.

"Several times," Darrel said. "Stock up on water and fruit, when it's available."

"Where are you from?" Mickey asked.

"Originally, the States," Darrel said. "Most recently, Venezuela. That's where I met this lovable scoundrel." Darrel slapped Raphael on the shoulder.

Raphael smiled and nodded.

Travis and Darrel chatted about the island until the coffee was ready. Travis stood, poured three cups, and slid the steaming cups in front of Darrel and Raphael.

They drank their coffee and chatted about the island, the weather, and far away destinations. Mickey interjected a few times, but mostly remained quiet. Still standing.

Darrel drained his cup, set it down, and stood up. "Well, we better take advantage of the morning and get to those repairs."

Raphael stood up beside him.

Travis stood and shook their hands again. "Presuming we're lucky with today's fishing, hope you can join us for dinner."

"That would be nice," Darrel said, as he turned to leave.

Raphael took another long look at Mickey and then followed Darrel out the door.

When they were back to their dinghy, Mickey leaned closer to Travis. "What do you think?"

Travis watched as Darrel and Raphael got into the boat and shoved off. He then turned to Mickey and locked eyes. "Wouldn't trust them as far as I could throw them."

"Why did you invite them to dinner?"

"Like they say, keep your friends close; keep your enemies closer."

Mickey nodded as she watched Darrel and Raphael row out to their cruiser.

"Let me clean this mess up, and then we'll get to fishing while it's still relatively cool."

Mickey pondered Darrel and Raphael while she waited for Travis. She had been hoping for a way off the island since she arrived. Darrel and Raphael had a boat capable of delivering her to Hawaii, if they were willing. Darrel seemed nice enough. Raphael was just plain creepy. She thought about Travis's opinion of them, and she thought about her need to report Roundabout's sinking. Mickey was well past her arrival time in Samoa. She told Janet she would call upon her arrival. Certainly she would be worried by now. Should she just wait until the authorities showed up looking for Roundabout, or take a chance on a boat ride off the island? That was not a decision she had to make this minute. There was time. A couple of days, at least.

Mickey followed Travis down to their dinghy tied up on the beach. She rowed out to the cat, where they gathered the fishing gear. She then rowed past the cruiser on her way to the channel.

From what she could see, the cruiser looked like it was in pretty good shape. From her size, Mickey guessed the boat probably had the requisite saloon and galley, probably three berths, and two heads. What she'd really like to do is get a look on board while Darrel and Raphael were gone. But with the island being so small, she doubted she would ever get that chance. She wondered what kind of repairs they were making. They weren't on deck; something down below. Could be anything. Boats are always breaking.

Mickey rowed, but kept her attention on the cruiser. Soon they hovered over their usual spot.

Travis threw the anchor out and then handed the rod and reel to Mickey. "Do your magic. I'll be right here." He slouched back against the inflated side of the boat and pulled his wide brim hat lower over his forehead.

Mickey turned to the open ocean, adjusted the reel, and tossed the lure out about twenty degrees off the reef. The current would move it toward the reef as she reeled.

She thought about the last time she and Susan went fishing with their dad. Mickey was around ten; Susan was two years older. They were in a small bass boat on Cedar Creek Lake, near Dallas. It was one of her dad's favorite fishing lakes. Fishing was great, at first. They caught several of the bass the lake was noted for. Mickey even caught one, the largest she had ever caught up to that point. She remembered her excitement at reeling the fish in and her dad scooping it up in the net. After a couple of hours the fish stopped biting, and they mostly sat quietly. She remembered giggling with Susan and her dad telling them to hush. She remembered that he was quieter than normal, more serious. He hadn't said much all day when finally he turned to face the two girls. *I need to tell you girls something*. Mickey would remember those words forever. His expression showed it was something important. Even so, she did not expect the news that he and their mother would be living apart. And that the girls would be staying with their mother. He seemed sad, but determined. He tried to explain that nothing would change between him, Mickey, and Susan. And at first, it didn't. They saw him nearly every weekend. But then the intervals became longer. Mickey saw him for the last time when she was fourteen. Her mother never remarried. She turned sick and died shortly after Mickey finished college and got her first full-time job. Susan had married Thomas by then. Mickey grew to resent her dad more and more until by the time she started working, she didn't care if she ever heard from him again. She wondered now if that was true, or if it was just a way to relieve the pain. Mickey remained close to Susan even though they lived far apart—Mickey in New York and Susan in California. Eventually, they learned that their dad had died in some Godforsaken place on the other side of the world. Susan was the only family she had left at that point. Which was why Mickey thought it was important to report Susan's loss as soon as possible.

***

With two cans of green beans from Travis's boat and Darrel's contribution of red potatoes, Mickey whipped together the two sides, and the baked tuna they had caught that day. She placed the food on the table between the three men, who were drinking beers also provided by Darrel. Mickey placed a filet and some of the sides on her plate as the men continued to talk about boats and their travels.

"Better eat it while it's hot," Mickey said.

The three men stopped talking at once, glanced at Mickey, and then scooped food onto their plates. They started talking again while they drank and munched.

Mickey was mostly left out of the conversation since she had never been to any of the places they talked about—ports in places from South America to Indonesia. From the conversation, Mickey gathered that Darrel and Raphael had been around. As they continued to jabber, Mickey started to wonder how the two men financed their travels.

When the sun dropped below the horizon and the light began to fade, Travis lit his lantern. And the conversation and beers continued.

It was well into the evening when Darrel drained the last of his beers, slammed the empty on the table, and stood. "I guess we should head back to the boat." He looked over at Raphael.

Raphael had not said that much all night, and after several beers, he said even less. He just gawked. At Mickey.

Mickey tried her best to ignore his stares. She focused on the conversation between Travis and Darrel, interjecting a question occasionally, trying not to sound stupid.

Darrel slapped Raphael on the back. "Let's go my friend. We have an early morning." He looked at Travis and Mickey. "More repairs. Didn't get it all done today."

"What's the problem?" Travis asked.

"Clogged lines from the head and the alternator isn't charging the batteries," Darrel said. "But we've got a handle on it. Should be done tomorrow."

Travis nodded. "See you in the morning then."

Darrel smiled, nodded, and then guided Raphael out of the building and into the night.

When Mickey heard them getting into their dinghy, she turned to Travis. "Has your opinion of them changed at all? Darrel seems nice enough."

"No," he said. He turned face to face with Mickey. "Stay close to me while they're around."

CHAPTER 15

The next morning Mickey entered the main building and joined Travis at the counter where he was putting the finishing touches on his famous porridge.

"Any sign of Darrel and Raphael?" Mickey asked.

Travis dropped pieces of banana and papaya into the oats as he nodded toward the lagoon. "Already at work on their boat. I saw them on deck earlier. Now they're down below."

"What do we have planned for today?" Mickey asked.

Suddenly Travis winced and bent over slightly. He placed a hand on his abdomen.

"Are you okay?"

Travis took several deep breaths as he stood up straight. "I'll be fine."

Mickey helped him to a chair.

"Don't fuss," Travis said. "I'll be fine. Just need to catch my breath."

"The pain is a lot worse isn't it?"

Travis looked into her eyes. "Some. I'll be fine."

"Coming here alone was a bad idea," Mickey said. "What did you expect to do when the pain got unbearable?"

"I wasn't thinking about the pain at the time." Travis took several more deep breaths and regained his composure. "I'm feeling better."

Mickey moved to the counter, finished adding the fruit to the bowls, and sat them on the table with two spoons. She sat down across from Travis. "You need to eat something."

Travis nodded, blinked a couple of times slowly, and picked up the spoon.

Mickey glanced out to the lagoon. "Let's skip fishing today. Looks like rain, anyhow."

Travis nodded as he stirred the fruit in with the oats. He then took a small bite and chewed.

Mickey stared at him a few moments more, and then took a bite, chewed, and swallowed. "You should rest today."

Travis nodded and then flashed a weak smile. "I'll lie down a while. Didn't get much sleep last night."

***

Mickey was putting dishes away when she heard the jiggle of plastic water jugs banging together. She glanced around and saw Darrel carrying two five-gallon jugs in each hand, walking toward the main building. When he got closer Mickey saw that he was smiling. His hair looked less wild than before and he wore cleaner clothes. He looked like he had taken a shower. "Morning," he said, as he stood outside the screen door with the jugs still in hand.

"Good morning," Mickey said. "Water day?"

"Yep. I elected myself to get started. Raphael is still working out some kinks on the boat."

"Will you be able to fix the problems?"

"Absolutely," Darrel said. "It just takes time. Working in cramped spaces isn't easy."

Mickey nodded. "I can give you a hand with the water if you want."

"Much appreciated," Darrel said. He looked around the building and then the grounds. "Where's Travis?"

"Not feeling well."

"Nothing serious, I hope."

Mickey clenched her jaw, but said nothing.

Darrel motioned his understanding with his chin. "Anything we can do?"

"Not really," Mickey said, as she started toward the door. "Let me give you a hand with the water."

She stepped out of the door and took two of the jugs. "How much do you need?"

"It will take several trips," Darrel said, as he turned toward the main square.

Mickey fell in next to him. "When the researchers are here, they apparently run a generator and a pump for the water," Mickey said. "But the generator room is locked and there's no gas."

"We have a few gallons of gas for the dinghy," Darrel said, "but we're trying to conserve. Which is why we've been rowing." He looked toward the shower building. "The last time I was here, there was a gravity-fed faucet on the outside of the shower building."

"Still there," Mickey said. "And it works."

Darrel positioned the jug under the faucet and turned on the flow. It was slow, but steady. "This is going to take awhile."

Mickey leaned against the wall next to the faucet. "Which state?"

Darrel looked at her with a confused look.

"You said you were from the states."

"Oh. Maryland. Outside of Annapolis. What about you?"

"Originally Texas, outside of Dallas. But now I work in New York. The city."

"How do you like it?" Darrel asked.

"Challenging work. The city is fun, but it was a long way from my sister in LA."

"The sister you lost?"

Mickey nodded. "And my brother-in-law. They were my only family."

"I'm sorry to hear that," Darrel said. "And now you need to get back to Hawaii."

"Right. I left word at work where I was going. They know by now that I didn't show up in Samoa, as planned. They must be looking for the boat."

Darrel nodded. "Big ocean. They'd start in Samoa and work back. Could take a while."

Mickey shuffled her feet a bit. "Are you headed toward Hawaii?"

Darrel paused for a moment, thinking. He then looked over at Mickey. "We didn't really have a destination in mind when we set out. I suppose Hawaii is as good as any."

"Would you have room for an extra passenger?"

"Can always make room. What about Travis?"

"He won't leave the island. I'll get help for him once I reach Hawaii."

Darrel smiled at Mickey. "We should be able to pull out in the morning."

Mickey nodded. "Thank you."

Darrel placed a hand on Mickey's shoulder. "It will be fine."

Darrel began ferrying the full water jugs to his dinghy and out to the cruiser, while Mickey continued filling. She probably could have taken the opportunity to get a look at Darrel's boat, but decided to hang close to Travis in case he needed something.

She looked toward his cabin and wondered if he was in a lot of pain lying there. When the second of her two jugs was full, she twisted the faucet off and walked to Travis's cabin. She peered through the screen door into the darkness inside. She could see him lying on the bunk, on his side. She opened the door, trying to be as quiet as possible, but the sound of the door opening caused Travis to look up. Mickey smiled and continued into the room. "How you feeling?"

"Better, I think," Travis said, as he laid his head back on the pillow. "What have you been up to?"

"Helping Darrel fill water jugs," she said. "He'll be pulling out in the morning."

Travis nodded.

"I think I need to go with him. He's agreed to take me to Hawaii."

Travis looked up and shook his head slightly. "I don't have a good feeling about him and Raphael."

"I feel the same about Raphael, but Darrel actually seems okay."

"Wolf in sheep's clothing," Travis said. "You can't trust either one of them."

"I can't just wait here another five or six months until the researchers come back. I'm not sure we even have enough food for that long. Plus, you need help, whether you think so or not. I can't watch you go through the pain. And I suspect it will get a lot worse."

Travis took in a deep breath and let out a slow exhale.

"I will bring help back for you. And I need to let people know about my sister and brother-in-law. He had a business. His partners need to know."

Travis relaxed his head into the pillow and closed his eyes. "I don't think it's a good idea," he mumbled.

"I'll let you rest," Mickey said, as she stood. She paused a moment and looked down at the old man. Only two months earlier he seemed strong and vibrant. Now he appeared weak and fragile. It would be impossible for Mickey to watch him suffer without doing something. A few days on Darrel's boat seemed the only option.

***

In the afternoon, Mickey rowed Travis's dinghy toward the catamaran. Off to the left, she gazed at the cruiser, fifty yards away. Both of the men were apparently below deck. Working on the repairs, Mickey presumed.

She tied up at the starboard sugar scoop, hopped aboard, and immediately scrambled down the stairs to the galley. She opened the various lockers in search of canned food that would be easy for Travis to prepare while she was gone. Spam, canned tuna, and soup would be perfect. She opened the lockers, rummaged through the contents, and closed the lockers. She found dry goods along with canned vegetables and fruit, but not the protein high foods she wanted. Knowing that every available nook and cranny was used to store food, she stepped into the starboard berth, and checked the lockers. She found extra line, paper charts, and all sorts of nautical paraphernalia, but no canned provisions.

She then popped up the ladder, over to the port hull, and started checking lockers. In a locker below the pass through berth she hit the jackpot. She found a variety of soups, along with canned meats. She tried to calculate the number of days it would take to reach Hawaii and then return. Palmyra included a dirt airstrip built by the navy and maintained by the researchers. Getting back would be no problem. Mickey would charter a plane if she had to. Getting there would take some time.

The cruiser could maintain a steady speed, much faster than a sailboat, but it would still take days. Mickey didn't know how fast the boat could average, but just to be safe, she figured ten knots. That would be two-hundred and forty miles per day. Mickey figured five days, plus a sixth to get back. A week. A week seemed like a long time for Travis to be in pain, but there wasn't much she could do about it.

She sorted the food for a total of seven days and then gathered it together on top of the bunk. She then looked around at the other lockers wondering what other food might be on board. She started opening lockers until she had made her way into the owner's cabin. In there she found Travis's clothes, shoes, and a bunch of other stuff needed to operate a boat on the high seas. She also found a small wooden box, about the size of a cigar box, only twice as deep.

She thought for a moment about opening the box to see what was inside. Could be personal stuff, in which case Travis wouldn't like it much. But the temptation was too much.

Mickey sat the box on the bunk and lifted the lid. She pulled out the contents and placed them on the mattress beside the box. The items included a stack of photographs, most yellowed with age. They depicted a young man with dark hair, a young woman, probably his wife, and a little girl. The little girl reminded Mickey of herself at that age, probably nine or so. They looked happy together in their various poses, especially the little girl. She had no idea of the changes that were about to occur.

There were also photos of a younger Travis, during his obvious world travels. One showed him decked out in climbing gear and a parka, standing in the snow at the top of some high mountain. Another showed him standing with a bunch of natives. The surroundings looked like Africa. There were many others.

Mickey set the photos to the side and picked up a stack of letters, still in their envelopes. They were all tied together with a piece of twine. Mickey untied the bow and sorted through the envelopes. None appeared to have been mailed.

She opened the top envelope and pulled out the folded pages. She opened the pages and read the first line. *Dear Clara.*

The date scribbled at the top indicated it had been written a year earlier. She opened the next envelope down, unfolded the pages, and checked the date. It was dated a year earlier still. She went back to the top letter, apparently the last one he had written, and started reading.

In it, he described events in his life over the prior year—the places he had been and the things he had done. At the end, he touched on his regret for leaving his daughter, and he apologized for any harm he had done.

Mickey opened the next letter down, read it, and then read the third letter. They all followed the same theme. He described his life for the prior year and closed with an apology for leaving. There was nothing in any of the letters about him being sick.

Mickey picked up the top envelope, flipped it over, and looked at the address block. It was addressed to *Clara Stevens,* at an Orlando address. There was no return address.

Mickey put the letters back in their envelopes, retied the bundle, and placed them and the photos back in the box. She closed the box and rested her hand on the closed lid. He had written all these letters to Clara, year after year, and never mailed any of them. She probably didn't know if he was alive or dead. Maybe she didn't care. But maybe she did.

Mickey returned the box to its locker, grabbed an empty canvas bag hanging on a hook on the wall, and returned to the pass through bunk. She loaded the cans of food into the bag and then made her way out to the deck and onto the dinghy. She untied the boat and started rowing back to shore. As she neared the cruiser, she decided to stop by and see how the repairs were going.

She tied up to the stern and stepped on the transom platform. Since there was no one in sight, she climbed aboard.

The cruiser, a trawler really, consisted of a short open deck in the stern and a ladder up to a second deck. From the second deck, there was another ladder leading up to a final, third deck. Mickey didn't see a wheel on the third deck and figured it was mainly for observation. Probably included sofas, chairs, and a lot of empty beer cans. Fishing would be from the open aft deck where Mickey stood. Mickey stepped along the port deck. She noted several hatches looking into cabins below the main deck. Amidship, there was a half-wood, half-glass door. Mickey peered inside at what was obviously a wheel house. Again, there was no one in sight. She eased the door open, stepped inside, and looked around. The wheel house occupied the front portion of the cabin and housed the helm and all the instruments. The rear portion of the wheel house included a large table with a sofa around it. Behind the table there was a short companionway and a ladder to the deck below.

Mickey took a moment to admire the workmanship of the boat. There was plenty of rich colored wood. Mickey especially liked the way it was laid out. She imagined the galley was down the ladder, and the berths and heads were forward of the galley, just below the helm. The entire wheel house was completely enclosed with windows and expensive wood. It was a nice boat.

There was still no one in sight, but Mickey did hear muted voices coming from below. She was about to call out when she stopped herself and gazed around the cabin again.

The cabin was cluttered with stuff. Some of it looked new. All of it looked expensive. There were rods and reels, guns, art pieces, musical instruments, and even suitcases. There were many more items than anyone would need on a boat in the middle of the ocean.

Mickey picked up a rifle from the sofa. She didn't know much about guns, but this one seemed to be in good shape. No rust. She put it back where she got it and then turned a three-sixty as she scanned the other items. It suddenly dawned on her why Darrel and Raphael were in the middle of the Pacific, *cruising*. They were modern-day pirates. Had to be. It was the only thing that would explain all the stuff.

The muffled voices were still coming from below when Mickey back-stepped out the wheel house door, tip toed down the deck, and climbed back into the dinghy. Her bare feet and light frame gave no indication of her having been on the boat. She pushed away and then began rowing, being careful how she worked the oars to not make any noise. She kept her eye on the cruiser as she made her way back to the shore.

As she secured the dinghy to a palm tree and retrieved the food, she wondered what this meant for her plans to travel with Darrel and Raphael to Hawaii. Being pirates didn't necessarily put her in any danger. So far Darrel had done nothing that would concern her. And neither had Raphael, except for his ogling. But that was nothing new for Mickey. She got that reaction from a lot of men. She considered whether she should mention her revelation to Travis. It would certainly confirm his wariness of the two men. It came down to two options: Go with Darrel and Raphael and take her chances, or stay behind, watch Travis suffer and probably die, and possibly run out of food waiting for the next ride. Given a vote, she was sure Travis would want her to avoid the two men. But her vote was the only one that counted.

CHAPTER 16

"I still don't think it's a good idea," Travis said, lying in his bunk. "Two strange men, alone on the open ocean. It's just not a good idea."

"I don't have much of a choice," Mickey said, sitting in a chair next to Travis's bunk. She glanced outside at the coming dawn and then back to Travis. "The food you brought won't last the months we may need to wait until the next person comes along. Plus, whether you like it or not, I'm coming back for you."

"That's not necessary, I'm feeling better," Travis said, as he tried to raise up. He winced and then laid back.

"I got you plenty of food from the boat," Mickey said. "Easy to prepare. It's in the main building. I'll be back before you know it."

Travis shook his head.

"I need to run. Darrel said they'd be pulling out first thing," Mickey said, as she started to rise.

Travis placed his hand on Mickey's knee and looked into her eyes. "Be careful."

"I will. You just take care of yourself. Don't forget to eat and drink."

Travis nodded. "Don't give either of them—," his words trailed off.

Mickey patted Travis's hand. "I understand." She stood up. "I'll be back as soon as I can."

Travis nodded. "You know, you don't seem like a Mickey. You seem more like a Michelle. I've thought that since the day you told me your name."

Mickey paused. "I've always been called Mickey. My father called me Mickey Moo."

Travis closed his eyes and seemed to drift off. "Michelle," he mumbled. "It fits you better."

Mickey stepped to the door, took a final look back, and then exited the cabin. She eased the door shut and then walked off toward the lagoon. She met Darrel and Raphael coming up from the beach.

"We're ready to head out," Darrel said. "Are you still coming?"

"I am," Mickey said.

"Do you need help with your stuff?"

"What I'm wearing is all I have," Mickey said. She then stuck a finger through the hole in the front of her t-shirt. "The sooner I can get to Hawaii, the better."

"How's Travis?" Darrel asked. "We have room for him, too."

"Not so good," Mickey said. "That's another reason I need to get to Hawaii as soon as possible. He won't leave the island."

Darrel nodded, glanced at Raphael, and then motioned for Mickey to follow.

Raphael wore his perpetual smile.

Mickey fell in behind the two of them.

At the shore, Darrel walked straight to Travis's dinghy and grabbed hold of the rope. "We should pull this up farther," he said, as he pulled the boat well into the sand. He then retied the rope.

Raphael jumped into their dinghy and immediately took a seat between the oars.

Darrel held Mickey's hand while she stepped aboard and then pushed off. He waded through the water, hopped aboard, and motioned for Raphael to start rowing.

Raphael rowed the rubber boat to the stern of the cruiser, where Darrel tied off and then helped Mickey onto the platform.

With everyone aboard, Darrel and Raphael pulled the dinghy to the starboard side of the cruiser, pulled the rubber boat onto the deck, and secured it in front of the wheelhouse, near the bow.

While Raphael entered the wheelhouse, Darrel joined Mickey in the aft section. "Follow me," he said, as he led her down the port deck and through the wheelhouse door. When she entered, he motioned with his arm. "Home away from home... for a few days. I think you'll find this more comfortable than the island."

"And a lot more fun, too," Raphael said from behind the wheel.

Mickey picked up on the glare Darrel shot toward Raphael.

Raphael smiled and turned back to the wheel.

"Let me show you around," Darrel said, as he motioned Mickey farther into the cabin.

Mickey hesitated a moment, but then followed. The first thing she noticed was that all the stuff she saw before was gone. She figured they moved it all to a berth below deck. The other thing she noticed was how neat and orderly the room was. It was still a little dirty, but much better that what she saw the day before.

"Let me show you your berth and the galley," Darrel said, as he stepped around the table and down the ladder. The deck behind, and slightly below, the wheelhouse included the galley and another table with sofas, and two captains' chairs. He led Mickey around the table, down a ladder, and along a companionway. He opened the door to the first cabin on the port side. "You'll be in here," he said, as he swung the door open.

Mickey put one foot inside the cabin and looked around. There was a set of bunk beds against one bulkhead, with a pass-through to a head. Mickey stepped farther into the cabin, ran her hand over the sheet on the top bunk, and then stepped into the head. She noted that it was amazingly clean, considering it was on a boat with two guys. The head included an electric toilet, a sink, and a shower. There was a towel hanging on a hook next to the sink. Mickey looked around again and then back to Darrel. "Nice."

"Let me show you the galley," he said, as he led her out of the room. Back in the companionway he pointed to the closed door, a little forward and on the starboard side. "I'm in there. Raphael usually stays close to the helm, even when he's off duty."

"Does she have an autopilot?" Mickey asked.

"She does," Darrel said, as he led her back down the hall and back up the ladder. He crossed the saloon and then stepped back into the galley.

Mickey looked around at the various appliances and lockers. Surprisingly, the galley, too, was fairly clean. She heard the engines turn over and then settle into a low rumble.

"Need two people to get through the channel," Darrel said, as he motioned up with his chin.

Mickey nodded and then followed him up the ladder and into the wheelhouse. She took a seat at the table as Darrel stepped behind the wheel.

Raphael went out the door and toward the bow.

Darrel waited for Raphael to get into position and then pushed a button for the electric windlass.

Mickey stood up and looked through the forward windows at Raphael as he sprayed the chain with a water hose as the anchor came up. With the anchor secure, Raphael made his way along the deck and back into the wheelhouse.

Darrel eased the throttles forward a bit and turned the wheel until the bow was lined up with the channel.

Mickey suddenly had an uneasy feeling and wondered if she was doing the right thing. Maybe Travis was right. Maybe she should have just waited on the island. In the long run, it might be safer. But it wouldn't help Travis's situation. She took several deep breaths, rubbed a hand over her abdomen, and sat back down at the table.

Darrel looked over at Mickey, smiled and winked. He then turned back forward as he eased toward the channel. His gaze constantly shifted from his instruments to the window and the approaching channel. As he neared the channel, he backed off a bit on the throttles.

Raphael, who had been watching out the front windows as Darrel maneuvered the large craft, suddenly turned his head and smiled at Mickey. While maintaining the smile, he stepped over to the table and took a seat next to her. "This is going to be a fun trip," he said, as he placed his hand on Mickey's knee.

Mickey tensed and glanced at Darrel, who seemed to be occupied with the approaching channel. Without saying anything, Mickey picked up Raphael's hand and moved it away from her leg.

"Don't be that way," Raphael said. He then snickered. "We can all be friends."

Mickey quickly slid around the sofa and came to her feet at the other end of the table, facing Raphael.

Darrel apparently caught sight of the movement and glanced over at Raphael. "I need you on the bow."

Raphael stood and quickly moved toward Mickey as though he was going to place his arm around her neck.

Mickey ducked his arm and then hurried over and stood next to Darrel, while still facing Raphael.

Raphael snickered again and sauntered toward Mickey.

Darrel glanced at Raphael approaching and then at Mickey, while keeping his hands on the wheel. "Did you really have to start this now," he said to Raphael. He huffed. "Just lock her below and then get out to the bow."

Mickey froze at Darrel's words and slowly turned to face him.

Darrel kept his focus ahead. "Sorry, Mickey, but out here you're a valuable commodity. Your boat sinking with all hands just makes it that much easier for you to disappear."

With her back to Raphael, Mickey glanced out the front windows and saw that the boat was about a quarter of the way through the channel. "Travis was right about both of you."

"From what I saw of his condition, Travis won't be around much longer to worry about it."

Mickey then felt Raphael's hand on her shoulder and then felt it slide down her chest. He wasn't careful about avoiding her breasts. His other hand then took hold of the opposite shoulder.

Mickey spun around and kneed Raphael in the groin. He immediately groaned and bent over at the waist, losing his grip.

She sprinted for the door, bolted out to the deck, and back to the stern. She looked around to get her bearings and realized the boat was about halfway through the channel and would be in the open ocean in a matter of seconds. Without looking back, she took off running aft, put one foot on the transom, and leapt into the water. She glanced back at the boat and saw Raphael standing at the stern.

She turned her head toward the shore, kicked her feet, and began taking overhead strokes. She swam against a slight current heading out of the channel.

Given her time on the island, she had learned something about the tides and knew that she was on the cusp of low tide. The current would be increasing, and it wouldn't be in her favor. She increased her overhead strokes, glancing back at the cruiser with each turn of her head.

The boat continued toward the open ocean, with Raphael still standing in the stern. Mickey then saw him walk back to the wheelhouse and enter. She watched as the boat continued out of the channel, into the open water, and begin a turn. She heard the motors rev. She glanced back and saw the boat heading back for the channel.

Mickey continued her strokes toward the beach as she started thinking about what to do once she reached land. The island was small. She could try to hide, but eventually she would be found. She thought about Travis, but then realized there was little he could do in his weakened state. Even if he were at his best, there were two of them. Her mind raced until her mind blurred. She stopped trying to figure out what to do and focused on just reaching the beach.

Fifty yards from the white sand, Mickey heard the boat's motors rev louder and realized they had cleared the channel. She glanced back and further realized the boat would be on her before she got to the beach.

With limp noodles for arms and legs, she forced herself to increase her strokes. She struggled to breathe, since her large gulps of air were often accompanied with salt water. She choked as she tried to spit the water out between inhales.

The idyllic life of the tropical island's sun, surf, and perfect weather had suddenly turned into a nightmare. Images of being sold into sex slavery flashed through her mind. She imagined the greasy, dirty, fat men pawing her with their disgusting hands. She thought of their foul breath and their wicked expressions as they glared at Mickey's naked body. She'd rather be dead.

Based on the sound of the engines, without looking back, she knew the boat had continued past the spot where they previously had anchored. Darrel was pressing on toward her and the beach. Just as Mickey thought of the little outcrops of corral that dotted the areas of the lagoon closer to the island, some above the water, but some just below the surface, she heard a screech, like rock against fiberglass. As her hands touched the sand on her down stroke and she shifted her feet to run rather than swim, she glanced back. The boat was practically on top of her as she sprinted on wobbly legs through the shallow surf. Then she heard the engines cut off and the boat's v-hull slide against the sand. Then she heard a splash.

As she ran toward the sand, she looked back to see Raphael only fifteen yards back, running hard through the water. She also saw Darrel on the bow in the process of jumping over the guard rail. It looked like Mickey wouldn't have a chance to hide, with them only seconds behind. She gulped air as she ran. Stress and anxiety coursed down the back of her neck and tried to freeze her limbs. Despite her fear, and the feeling of trying to move through quicksand, she willed her arms and legs to move. Just as she reached the beach, Raphael caught hold of her arm. She spun to get away, but his grasp was too much. She tried to use the fingers of the opposite hand to pry his hand off. When that didn't work, she tried scratching as she spun around. And then Darrel grabbed hold of her other arm. She screamed and bucked as she collapsed to the white sand, exhausted and out of breath.

CHAPTER 17

Raphael and Darrel jerked Mickey to her feet.

She stood on wobbly legs; her wet skin, hair, and clothes matted with sand.

"Let's get her back to the boat," Darrel said, as he began pulling Mickey in that direction.

A voice from the edge of the grass stopped everyone in their tracks. Everyone turned in unison.

"I'm actually feeling better this morning," Travis said in a calm voice. He stood, both hands behind his back, facing the three on the beach. "It appears she's changed her mind about leaving."

"Stay out of this old man... she's coming with us," Raphael raged. Spit flew from his mouth as he spoke.

Darrel let go of Mickey's arm and took two steps toward Travis. "There's no going back now, she's coming with us."

"I don't think so," Travis said. Travis winked at Mickey.

Raphael pushed Mickey to Darrel to hold and then stepped toward Travis. "You look like you're about to fall over, old man," he said, as he pulled the knife from the scabbard on his hip. He pointed the knife at Travis. "You should go lie down."

Mickey pulled against Darrel's grasp. Unable to get loose, she relaxed, glanced at the knife, and then looked at Travis. Given the odds, she figured Travis would end up dead and she would still end up as a sex slave. "It's okay, I'll go with them."

Darrel threw his head back, laughed, and then turned Mickey toward the boat. "Deal with him, Ralph."

Mickey struggled against Darrel's grip on her arms. "I said I would go, just leave him alone."

Darrel stopped, turned Mickey to face Travis, and paused for a moment as he stared at Travis. "Thought about it," he said, as he shook his head, "and decided against it." He then nodded at Raphael.

Travis brought his right hand out as he turned to face Darrel and Mickey. His hand held a black semi-automatic pistol. He pointed it at Darrel. "I really think she'd rather not go with you two. Let her go."

Darrel eyed the gun and then positioned his body more behind Mickey.

Raphael slowly lowered the knife as he glanced at Darrel.

Darrel nodded his chin subtly.

Almost imperceptibly, Raphael flicked his wrist, the movement was blurred by its speed.

Mickey screamed as she turned toward Travis.

The knife appeared almost magically in Travis's chest, right side, next to the breast bone.

Travis winced, stumbled back, and went down to one knee. Red began to spread from the entry point on Travis's t-shirt. Travis's right hand, with the gun, dropped.

Raphael smiled broadly and took a step toward Travis.

Suddenly two loud *booms* broke the relative silence. Raphael's feet planted as his head jerked back. And then, like a tall tree being cut down in the forest, Raphael fell back slowly, full length. His back hit the sand with a loud *whack*. Blood oozed from a single hole in his forehead.

With Darrel staring at Raphael and frozen in apparent disbelief, Mickey took the opportunity to twist herself from his grasp. She took two steps through the shallow water and dove for the sandy beach. Within a millisecond of her face plowing into the sand, she heard two more rapid *booms*.

She looked back at Darrel just in time to see him clutch his abdomen, bend over, and then crumple into the water. She then looked toward Travis and saw him drop the pistol, sink to the ground, and fall back into the grass. She called out his name as she leapt to her feet and darted to his side.

"Told you I wasn't leaving this island," he moaned.

Mickey lifted the bottom edge of Travis's t-shirt and used it to put pressure against the wound. "Tell me what to do, should I remove the knife?"

Travis smiled, blinked slowly one time, and let out a long exhale. "It doesn't matter. Either way, I won't survive."

"Can you make it to the shade?" Mickey asked, as she tried to lift his shoulder.

Travis winced as he tried to rise up. With Mickey's help, he got to his feet and staggered to the nearest tree. He plopped down with his back against the trunk.

Mickey renewed her pressure on the wound and shook her head. "You should have stayed in bed."

"No, I did exactly what needed doing," he said. "Now you can go and live your life."

Mickey looked back at Raphael on the beach and Darrel in the water. "I guess you learned to shoot during your travels."

Travis glanced at the two bodies. "I was never that good, especially the forehead shot. Like they say, it's better to be lucky than to be good."

Mickey wiped away at the tears with her free hand. "I certainly didn't expect my time on the island to end this way. I would have come back with help for you."

Travis winced again as he tried to shift his back against the tree. "I know you would have. It's better this way. I didn't have a chance. But you do. Take the cat. Sail it to Hawaii. And then get on with your life. To truly live, you have to take risks. You're much stronger than you think. Live confidently. Don't fall victim to insecurity."

Mickey nodded as she wiped away at more tears. She closed her eyes. She wanted to tell him that he had been more like a father to her than her own father. She wanted to thank him for saving her life, but mere words didn't seem adequate. She wanted more time with him so she could express how much she appreciated all that he had done. She wiped the tears, opened her eyes, and opened her mouth to speak. But then she closed her mouth without saying anything.

He was gone.

***

Mickey stood with one hand on the end of the shovel handle, at the edge of the compound. She stared at the three mounds of dirt, but focused on the one separate from the other two. It was the only mound with a cross made of two limbs.

"I'm sorry, Travis," she said, "that you have to lie here next to these assholes."

She bowed her head for a few moments more. She then picked up the shovel and walked toward the main building. She stopped halfway and gazed at the lagoon. Her eyes hovered for a moment on the cruiser close to the beach, and then out to the catamaran, and then back to the cruiser. The cruiser sat a little lower in the water than before and was cocked to one side. *Probably damaged from the coral strike*, she thought. That left her no choice but to use the catamaran for her trip to Hawaii.

She turned and scanned the compound, from the main building, to the cabins, to the showers. With Travis gone, the whole place gave her an eerie feeling. She looked to the midday sun. The rest of the day would give her time to prepare for her voyage. She would leave the next morning, presuming she could find the gas Darrel mentioned.

Mickey continued on, returned the shovel to the side of the main building, and then walked back to the beach and entered the water. She rinsed the sand from her arms and face as she waded around to the rear of the cruiser. She pulled herself up on the transom's platform and then stepped into the stern.

Despite having been on the boat twice before, until that moment she had not noticed the six five-gallon jerry cans gathered and roped together in one corner. She twisted the cap off each of the cans and sniffed the contents. Four of the cans were full to the brim with diesel. The fifth can was empty. The sixth smelled like gasoline, filled nearly to the top.

She nodded with satisfaction as she stood up and stepped off toward the wheelhouse. Upon stepping through the doorway she instantly got a sense of foreboding. This is where, only a few hours earlier, she learned of Darrel's and Raphael's intent to sell her into slavery. But not before they each had their fill during the trip. She shuddered at the thought of either one of them touching her. She then wondered how many other women or girls had fallen victim to Darrel's charms. She had no doubt that he got exactly what he deserved.

She took a deep breath and looked around the cabin. She tried to think of what she might need on her voyage on the catamaran. At an average speed of five knots, it would take nine days to reach Hawaii. And there was a good chance she would not be able to average five knots. The trip could end up taking two weeks, or more. She would need enough food for that long, plus a little extra. And she needed easy to prepare food; little or no cooking. She thought of the food she had gathered for Travis. She would take that, but she needed more. She also needed water. There was plenty of fresh water in the compound, but she needed containers. Plastic bottles. She took another deep breath and then stepped down the ladder into the galley.

She searched every locker and pulled out food items as she went—mostly canned fruits and vegetables. She found a few cans of tuna, sardines, and some potted meat. She also found several boxes of crackers, a couple of packages of oatmeal cookies, two blocks of cheddar cheese, and a bag of Snickers bars in the refrigerator. Most importantly, she found ten one-gallon jugs of water. She gathered everything together on the counter. She then looked around for something to put the items in.

Seeing nothing in the galley, she went to the lower deck where the berths were located. She popped her head in her designated berth, expecting it to contain nothing of interest. She was right. She closed the door and went to Darrel's cabin, the one he pointed to earlier that day. She opened the door, peered inside, and then cautiously stepped in. The items of high value she had seen in the wheelhouse during her initial reconnoiter were all there, plus more. Mostly guns, all kinds of pistols and rifles. There was also an assortment of electronics—portable stereos, iPads, laptops, and even musical instruments. Every space was crammed. She couldn't imagine needing any of the items, so she stepped out and was about to close the door when she stopped. She stepped back in and examined the various firearms.

She knew very little about guns, but having one on board with her might not be a bad idea. It was always possible she would run into more Raphaels. The semi-automatic pistols and rifles all seemed too complicated. But she had gone to the range one time with a previous boyfriend and watched as he fired a revolver. That seemed easy enough. Open the cylinder, slide in the bullets, close, point, and pull the trigger. She found a shiny silver one with a short barrel that looked simple enough. She picked it up and opened the cylinder. It was loaded with five rounds. She had to look close to read the lettering on the back of the bullets. *Three five seven*. Now she just needed some more bullets. She shuffled through several boxes until she found two that were marked *three five seven*. She took them both, picked up the gun, and stepped out of the cabin.

There was one more cabin she had not looked in. She shifted the gun and two boxes of ammo to one hand and then turned the knob on the door to the third cabin. She pushed the door open and stepped inside. With her hand still on the door knob, she froze. Stunned. What she saw was the last thing she expected to see. She blinked several times to make sure she was seeing what she was seeing.

CHAPTER 18

A woman. Actually, a girl. She couldn't be older than her middle to late teens. She had dark skin and long, black hair. She was completely nude, gagged, with her wrists and ankles tied to the bunk bed. Her legs were stretched apart. *Another victim intended for the sex slavery market.* The girl didn't stir when Mickey entered. *She must be dead,* was Mickey's first thought. Dead or alive, she couldn't leave her there.

Mickey inched across the deck to the side of the bunk. The girl's eyes were closed. But then Mickey noticed that her breasts gently rose and fell. Mickey leaned closer and placed two fingers on the girl's forearm. Her skin was warm and moist from sweat.

Suddenly, the girl blinked her eyes open and immediately recoiled. Her eyes wide with fear. She struggled against the ropes as she wiggled back and forth on the bare, disgusting mattress.

"It's okay," Mickey said, as she placed her hand on the girl's shoulder. Mickey sat the gun and two boxes of ammo on the deck and immediately pulled the gag out of the girl's mouth.

The girl screamed and struggled more against the ropes.

"It's okay," Mickey said again, "they're gone. Those two men will never harm you again."

The girl calmed a bit as she stared into Mickey's eyes.

Mickey went to work on untying the girl's restraints. "Do you speak English?" Mickey asked, as she glanced up at the girl.

"A little," the girl said in a heavily accented voice full of fear.

"My friends call me Mickey. What is your name?" Mickey released the girl's right arm from the rope. Her wrist was red and swollen.

The girl recoiled again as Mickey reached across to untie the left arm. "What is your name?" Mickey asked again.

"Elena," the girl mumbled.

When Mickey finally released the girl's left arm, the girl used both hands to cover herself as she pressed her back against the bulkhead. She watched as Mickey undid the knots holding her feet.

"Where the men?" Elena asked.

Mickey stopped fiddling with the ropes and stared at the girl. "They're dead and buried. They won't hurt you anymore." She then resumed her work. Mickey could feel some of the tension in Elena's legs dissipate as the words apparently sunk in.

With both feet free, Elena pulled her feet close to her as she curled into a fetal position.

Mickey looked around the room for anything Elena could wear. She spotted a small pair of shorts and a t-shirt. Both were soiled beyond usability. Mickey looked for something else and came up with a man's large, black t-shirt that looked halfway clean. She handed the shirt to the girl and motioned for her to put it on.

Elena relaxed her position long enough to slip the shirt over her head and then pulled it tight, down past her thighs.

Mickey stuck out her hand to the girl. "Let's get you out of here."

Elena looked at Mickey's hand and then gazed into her eyes.

Mickey smiled. "It's okay. You can leave."

Elena hesitated and then extended her right hand. She took hold of Mickey's fingers.

Mickey gently urged her off the bed.

The girl followed Mickey's lead and stepped to the deck. She stood on pencil-thin legs for a moment and then took a step as Mickey pulled her toward the door. Together they went out of the door and down the passageway.

The girl's head darted back and forth as though she expected Darrel or Raphael to jump out at any time.

Mickey led her down the corridor, up the ladder to the galley, up to the wheelhouse, and then out on deck.

"Where is this?"

"It's an island in the middle of the Pacific."

The girl nodded, but Mickey could tell she didn't really understand.

"How long have you been on the boat?" Mickey asked.

"Many days," Elena said, as she took a few steps toward the bow.

"Back this way," Mickey said, as she gently pulled her toward the stern. "We can get off the boat easier this way." The girl turned and followed Mickey as she led her to the stern, over the transom to the platform, and then into the water.

In the waist deep water, Elena immediately ducked the upper half of her body under the surface, and then rose up, spewing. She rubbed at her face and smoothed her long hair as she followed Mickey toward the shore. She pulled her wet t-shirt down over her thighs.

When they stepped up on the beach, Mickey pointed to the three mounds of dirt in the distance. "They won't bother you anymore."

Elena looked to where Mickey had pointed and then back to Mickey. "You did this?"

"No, my friend did." She pointed to the third mound. "He died to protect me, and you, it appears."

Elena nodded and then pulled away from Mickey. The girl ran to Darrel and Raphael's graves, stood for a moment, and then spit on the mounds. She then looked at the third grave, the one with the cross.

As Mickey stepped up beside her, she heard Elena say *thank you* in a barely audible voice. Mickey stood silently until Elena looked up. "You must be hungry and thirsty. I have food and water over here."

Elena turned to follow Mickey. She looked around as she walked. "Are there more people?"

"Nope. Just you and me."

Mickey led her to the main building and motioned for her to take a seat. She poured the girl a glass of water and opened a can of tuna. She mixed the tuna with some left over rice and placed the bowl between her hands on the table.

Elena gulped the water down and then started scooping the rice and tuna into her mouth with her fingers. She didn't bother using the spoon Mickey placed beside the bowl.

Mickey sat down across from her. "Where are you from?"

"An island," Elena said, as she swallowed one mouthful and scooped in another.

"And how old are you?" Mickey asked.

"Eighteen," she mumbled, as she chewed. She barely looked up from the bowl.

Mickey did not recognize the accent, but it sounded a little like French. Farther south, in French Polynesia, there were a ton of little islands that dotted the South Pacific. There was no way to know which might be her home. And besides, Mickey wasn't headed south, she was headed north. To Hawaii. If the girl agreed to go with her, the authorities could sort it out and get her medical treatment. There was no telling what Darrel and Raphael did to her, but it was probably painful and often.

Mickey wasn't sure whether she should bring up her departure the next day. That might be too much to grasp, given what the girl had just been through. Mickey decided to wait a little to break the news. For now the girl just needed some time to adjust while she ate and cleaned up. Mickey would show her the showers. She was in dire need of some soap.

"I need to go back on board the boat to find you something to wear," Mickey said. "Will you be okay here? I'll only be gone a few minutes."

Elena looked up from her half empty bowl and paused. "You be back?"

"Yes. I'll be right back."

Elena went back to eating while Mickey rose to her feet, left the main building, and walked to Travis's dinghy still tied to the palm tree.

She dragged the dinghy into the water and pulled it around to the stern of the cruiser. She tied it to the platform and then hopped aboard the cruiser. The first order of business was the gasoline. Without that, they would not be going anywhere. She dragged the jerry can to the transom and then struggled to get it over, and then down into the dinghy.

She then hopped back aboard and hurried into the wheelhouse. She looked around until she spotted a canvas bag near the helm. She emptied the contents, which included three sets of masks, snorkels, and fins, and then proceeded to the galley. She filled the bag with the food she had set out on the counter.

Two people will need double the food she previously calculated, so Mickey went back through the lockers and pulled out more cans. Mostly soups and cans of chili. She would be doing some cooking after all.

Getting the food and water to the dinghy took four trips. Standing in the dinghy after the last trip, she looked at the main building. She saw Elena walking around inside, apparently examining the appliances and cupboards.

Mickey climbed back on board the cruiser and proceeded below deck to find Elena some clothes. She searched every nook and cranny, but came up with only two small t-shirts, both clean, and a large wind breaker. She thought about the windbreaker, how it had likely been worn by Darrel or Raphael. Mickey sniffed the jacket and decided their stench would be too much for Elena. The t-shirts, both too small for either of the two men, were likely the property of some previous occupant of the boat.

Mickey kept the shirts, dropped the jacket on the floor, retrieved the pistol and ammo from the third berth, and deposited the five items in the dinghy. She climbed down, stepped into the water, and then pulled the dinghy back to shore and up on the sand. She stared back at the cruiser trying to think of anything the cruiser might additionally have that could be of use on the cat. In her mind she ticked off the various nautical instruments, and then went through the galley lockers, and then through the below deck cabins. She thought about taking one of the rifles, but then decided against it. A satellite phone would have been nice, but there wasn't one on board. Or, at least, she didn't find one. Satisfied she had everything of value, she returned to the main building, where she found Elena watching her through the screen.

Mickey entered the screen door and walked directly to the counter where the food she had left for Travis was gathered. "Can you give me a hand with this stuff?"

"What are you doing?" Elena asked.

Mickey stopped sorting cans and looked at the girl. She looked like she was about to cry. Mickey wanted to wait, to give her more time, but there was no more time. "We can't stay here. The food won't last. I'm taking the sailboat to Hawaii."

"Hawaii?"

"Yes. I will get you help there. The authorities will make sure you get back home."

"Why can't you take me home?"

"I don't know where home is for you. Plus, it's important that I get to Hawaii as soon as possible." Mickey took a few steps closer to Elena. "My boat sank, and I lost my sister. I have to report that, and I also have to report what happened here, with Darrel and Raphael. The police will want to investigate their activities."

A tear ran down Elena's cheek.

Mickey stepped closer and gently placed a hand on Elena's arm. "You will be safe with me. I'll make sure you get home."

Elena wiped the tears with her hand and then took hold of Mickey's hand. "We leave tomorrow?"

"Yes. First thing in the morning."

Elena nodded. "Your sister?"

"Yes. The boat we were on sank. My sister and brother-in-law did not survive. I washed up here. The man in the third grave saved my life."

Elena wiped the last of her tears. "Okay. I go with you."

"That's good," Mickey said, as she patted Elena on the arm. "Right now, why don't you follow me. I'll show you where you can clean up."

Elena gave a weak smile.

Mickey led her to the shower building, showed her the soap, and how to work the shower. She then waited outside. A few minutes later Elena stepped out, wearing the same large t-shirt, damp in spots, and her hair still wet. She looked better already. Her slender body and cute face would grow into a beautiful woman. She looked like the classic Tahitian.

"Are you from Tahiti?"

"No," Elena said, "but I know that island. My people talk of it."

Mickey nodded and smiled. "Can you help me take the food to the sailboat?"

Elena nodded and then followed Mickey.

Mickey worried about Elena's mental state. Being kidnapped from her home, held captive by two degenerates, and abused to an almost unimaginable level had to have taken a toll. She appeared a little jittery, jumped at the least little thing, but otherwise seemed okay. She was obviously ecstatic over being released. Seeing the two men dead and buried probably went a long way toward any vengeance she might feel. But still, it would be awhile before she returned to something approaching normal, if ever. She would certainly need counseling. Mickey couldn't provide that, but she could provide reassurance and a sense of security.

***

The sun was low in the western sky when Mickey and Elena finished loading the catamaran. They stowed the food in the boat's various lockers and then loaded a large stock of bananas and several papayas, along with as much water as they had containers, and the jerry can full of gasoline.

Mickey poured the gas into the boat's forward fuel tank and thought about checking the engines to make sure they would start. She decided against it. They would either start, or they wouldn't. She wanted to conserve the gas as much as possible. The next morning would decide their fate.

She showed Elena around the boat, the berth where she could sleep, and the head. She showed her how to work the toilet and explained that, under no circumstances, should paper ever be flushed. It would eventually clog the lines. She also explained that the shower used fresh water, which would be in short supply, so they probably would not be using the shower much. Mickey planned to bathe from the transom, just as she had done on Roundabout.

She led Elena back up to the helm and tried to explain the various instruments, especially the chart plotter and the autopilot. She explained that most of the power came from the two solar panels over the arch on the stern, and a small wind turbine mounted to one side. She pointed out the battery indicator and explained that power would be limited, so it was important to conserve as much as possible, especially on lighting at night. At the moment, the batteries were fully charged.

Mickey wasn't sure how much Elena understood, but was sure it would all come together for her. She seemed to catch on quickly.

Mickey looked to the open sea. There was still time to take the dinghy out to try for some fish. The activity would keep Elena's mind off of what happened to her. It would be better to keep her as busy as possible. She seemed willing to help. The girl wasn't lazy. Mickey would try to find ways to keep her mind and her hands occupied on the voyage to Hawaii. Fishing was one thing she could do, and it might as well start now, with Travis's rod and reel.

Mickey rowed Elena back out to the catamaran where they picked up the fishing rod, a couple of lures, and the dip net.

A few minutes later they were anchored just outside the channel. Just like Travis had shown Mickey, Mickey showed Elena how to work the reel and how to cast the line. Mickey flipped the reel out of gear, held the spool with her thumb, reached back, and cast the line. She then reengaged the gear and set the fish alarm clicker. Travis had already set the drag, so there was no reason to go into that mechanism. Mickey cast the line and reeled it in several times and then handed the pole to Elena.

At first she was clumsy with working her thumb on the spool and casting the line. Her first attempt plopped into the water only a few feet from the dinghy. Mickey showed her again, how to take a wide arc with her arm, instead of just flicking her wrist.

Mickey explained that the absolute most important thing to remember was to hold on to the pole, to not let it go for anything. If they lost the pole to the open ocean, they would be without a means to get fresh fish. It wouldn't be the end of the world, but it would deprive them of one of the few simple pleasures on what would be a long voyage.

Elena continued to practice casting the lure, reeling it in, and then doing it again. With each throw she got a little better, until finally she had her best cast yet. It went a good thirty or forty yards. Elena turned to Mickey with a wide grin.

Mickey smiled and nodded. "Excellent. Now we just need to hook a fish."

Elena reeled the lure in slowly and then cast the line again.

Mickey hoped she would actually hook a fish. It would do wonders. Then she started thinking about what would happen if she actually hooked a large tuna, something way too big to reel in.

Mickey was about to call it for the day when suddenly the tip of the rod bent and the line went tight. The fish on the other end nearly jerked the rod from Elena's hand, but she held on as the fish took the line out. Mickey jumped to her side and wrapped a hand around the rod for added support.

From the days of fishing Mickey and Travis had done over the past weeks, Mickey knew the fish on the other end was not too big. For Elena's benefit, Mickey pantomimed the motions necessary to pull the fish in. With an imaginary pole, Mickey pulled up and then let off the tension as she reeled. Then she pulled up again, and reeled.

Elena quickly got the hang of it and was making progress when suddenly the line went slack. She looked over at Mickey and raised her shoulders.

"It happens. It happens a lot. The fish got loose."

Elena's shoulders sank and her chin dipped as she reeled the empty lure to the end of the rod.

"It's getting late," Mickey said. "You can try again from the catamaran tomorrow."

Elena nodded and smiled.

Mickey pulled the anchor up and returned to shore.

In the evening, after eating from their stock of food and after Elena had fallen asleep in Travis's cabin, Mickey took the opportunity for one more shower. Still feeling the need to conserve water, she soaped down with the water off and then rinsed. And like she had done several times before, she washed her clothes in the sink and then hung them to dry on the clothes line before slipping into bed. Her mind remained active, trying to anticipate what she might need for the voyage. She ticked off all that she had done to prepare and then tried to think of anything else she needed to do. The sun had been down for several hours before she finally fell asleep.

CHAPTER 19

They used the spinnaker halyard and the winch to raise the dinghy out of the water. Elena, wearing Mickey's jean shorts and one of the clean t-shirts, turned the winch to lift the little boat as Mickey guided it over the guardrail and to a position in front of the mast. With the boat placed as best she could, Mickey went to the winch, released the line, and let it slide around the winch head until the dinghy was flat on the deck. Mickey then went forward, positioned the dinghy over the left trampoline, and lashed the boat securely. She stood up and gazed back at the cockpit with her hands on her hips.

Elena stepped from the cockpit to the deck and stared at Mickey. Her stance silently asked what Mickey was waiting for.

Mickey wondered about the trip and how Elena would do. At least she had something to wear. Mickey didn't mind giving up her shorts. They looked just as good on Elena. Mickey just hoped her yoga shorts and sports top held together. She would hate to show up in Hawaii wearing nothing. She finally took a deep breath, smiled at Elena in the distance, and then made her way toward the cockpit.

On Roundabout, Thomas always started the engines and then used the electric windlass to raise the anchor. This boat didn't have an electric windlass, just an under-deck roller, so Mickey was forced to crank the anchor up by hand.

With the anchor secured and the boat floating freely, it was time to find out if the engines would start. Mickey move to the wheel on the port side and pushed the two tilt buttons. She heard the motors drop into the down position. She then turned the key and pushed the start button for the starboard motor. She heard the engine turn over a few times and then fire to life. It settled into a low purr. The same with the port engine. Mickey exhaled a sigh of relief.

While Elena stood to her side, Mickey pushed the throttles forward and turned the wheel. Mickey had been on the island, and swam in the lagoon long enough, to know the location of every subsurface reef cropping that might be a threat to the cat. Mickey easily steered around each one on her way to the channel.

"Go up front and watch the water," Mickey said to Elena. "Let me know if I'm getting too close to the reef on either side."

Elena pointed to herself. "Go up front?"

"Yes. Watch the water. Yell out if I'm getting too close to the rocks on either side of the boat."

Elena nodded, left the cockpit, and went forward to the bow. She stood inside the bow rails on the port side, in front of the dinghy.

Mickey motored along at the slowest possible speed that provided helm control as she inched toward the channel opening. She was approaching another one of those fateful moments. If she scraped a hole in either hull, the trip would be over before it started. And they would truly be stuck on the island. She swallowed hard, trying to temper her anxiety. Because of the vibration of the motors, only she knew her hands were shaking.

She pressed on, lined the boat up as best she could, and kept one eye on Elena. The bow came up even with the coral, just below the surface, on both sides of the boat. Lucky for her, the lagoon was at a slack tide, which meant there was little current flowing through the channel. She hadn't planned her departure with the tide, it was just luck. Maybe it was a sign of success. Or maybe it was a false sense of security, lulling her to a doomed voyage. After all, the boat was tiny compared to Roundabout. The little cat wasn't meant for open ocean travel. Mickey shuddered at the prospect of running into a serious storm. Some of the waves she experienced on Roundabout, and floating in the ocean, would swamp the cat. Maybe she was making a mistake. Maybe she should remain on the island. It wasn't too late to turn back. In that moment of insecurity Mickey remembered what Travis had said. *Live confidently. Don't fall victim to insecurity.*

Mickey tightened her jaw and then tightened her grip on the wheel. She nudged the throttles forward just a hair.

The slight increase in speed improved the boat's steering. Three-quarters of the way through the channel, a sense of calm fell over her. Suddenly, she had no doubt about what she was doing and about her ability to sail the boat to Hawaii.

Her hands made minor steering adjustments as she kept her eyes forward. A few seconds later, they passed the end of the channel and entered the open ocean. The water went from light blue to dark blue as she passed over the outer reef edge. They were on their way.

Elena made her way back along the deck and joined Mickey under the hardtop. She watched

Mickey at the helm, probably wondering if she knew what she was doing.

Mickey glanced at Elena and smiled. She then turned back to the instruments and the open ocean ahead. *The blind leading the blind*, she thought.

As soon as she was safely in the darker water, she turned to starboard until the compass indicated she was headed north. She glanced at the wind indicator, which conveniently included the outline of a boat and a needle, indicating from which direction the wind was coming in relation to the boat's heading. A dial also provided wind speed. At the moment, the wind was off the boat's starboard bow at five knots. She expected the speed to increase once she completely cleared the island.

She continued motoring until she was several hundred yards northwest of the island. Sure enough, the wind increased to twelve knots off the starboard beam.

She turned the boat to starboard, into the wind, cut the engines, and pushed the lift buttons until the motors raised to the full up position. Mickey motioned for Elena to take the wheel and pointed to the compass. "Try to keep it on that heading."

"You want me to drive the boat?" Elena asked, fear etched on her face.

Mickey gave her a smile of reassurance and patted her on the shoulder. "Just keep it steady until I can raise the sails," she said, as she climbed out onto the deck, and then up on top of the hardtop.

She removed the mainsail cover and then looked up to make sure the halyard dropped directly from the top of the mast and was not wrapped around the shrouds, stays, or any other lines. She returned to the cockpit and took up the slack on the halyard and then locked it down in the clutch. She returned to the boom, removed all the sail ties, and then went back to the helm. She made sure the main sheet was free in the clutch and then wrapped the halyard line around the winch one time. She pulled on the line raising the sail until it became too hard to pull by hand. She wrapped the line around the winch two more times and then used the winch handle to hoist the sail up the mast. She stopped cranking when a black mark on the line came through the clutch. Travis had told her that the black line indicated the sail was fully raised. She then turned the boat to a north heading, adjusted the traveler, and trimmed the sail with the main sheet line.

The boat began moving through the water, picking up speed until the speed over ground topped off at five knots.

Next came the jib. She had deployed the jib numerous times on Roundabout, and a couple of times on the cat, with Travis supervising. She thought back to the process Travis had explained. According to Travis, it was important to keep tension on the furling line while she pulled on the jib's sheet line. That would ensure the furling line didn't get fouled. With that in mind, Mickey wrapped the jib sheet around the winch two times, took up the tension on the furling line, and pulled on the sheet line. She watched as the jib unfurled and began taking wind. Mickey looked over at Elena and told her to hold the wheel steady. Mickey fully deployed the jib and set the line. Satisfied both sails were trimmed the best she knew how, she returned to the helm.

She adjusted the chart plotter until Hawaii came on the screen. Her course line was a little to the left, so she turned the wheel slightly until the course was right on the mark. Her speed over ground increased to almost seven knots. She then set the autopilot and relaxed.

She turned to Elena who was staring at her with an expression of amazement, apparently mesmerized at all Mickey had just done. "I'll show you how. Once we get it set up, the boat really sails itself."

Elena nodded and blinked slowly, without saying anything, as she looked back at Palmyra Atoll.

Mickey followed her gaze and watched as the island grew smaller in the distance. Mickey sat on the cushioned seat behind the wheel and motioned for Elena to have a seat on the cushioned starboard seat, which doubled as a storage locker. "Are you okay?"

"Yes." She looked around the boat. "How long to Hawaii?"

"It's about a thousand miles," Mickey said, as she glanced at the speed indicator. "If we can average five knots, we should be there in about nine days."

"Nine days?" She looked around at the open ocean.

"Nine days," Mickey repeated. "We can stay busy with the boat and fishing. The time will go by quickly."

Elena nodded.

"Let's go below and get something to drink," Mickey said, as she stood up. She led Elena to the galley. "Make yourself at home here. Take anything you need." She pulled two bottles of water from a cupboard and handed one to Elena.

Elena opened her bottle, took a swig, and then wiped her mouth. "Boat drive alone?"

"It has an autopilot. But I'll still need to keep watch most of the time."

"What do I do?" Elena asked.

"Just help out around the boat; I'll show you. And conserve power and water." Mickey smiled as she motioned for Elena to follow. She led the girl back up to the cockpit. Mickey resumed her position behind the wheel; Elena sat at the open saloon table.

"Tell me about your home," Mickey said, as she scanned the open ocean ahead.

"Small island not too far from a bigger island."

"Do you go to school?"

"Yes. That's where I learn English. And my older brother helps me."

"Your English is very good. Mother and father?"

"Yes. My father is fisherman. He go out with a group from the island almost every day. They sell the fish on the big island."

"And your mom?"

"She at home." Elena began tearing up. "She will be worried where I am."

"When we get to Hawaii, I'm sure we can notify the authorities on your island. They will let your parents know you are okay."

Elena nodded.

"How did you come to be on the boat with the two men?"

"Early morning. I went down to beach to see sun. They talk to me, seem nice. But then they took me in little boat out to their bigger boat. I fight, but they much stronger."

"What about once you were on the big boat?"

Elena looked down at the table and fiddle with her plastic water bottle.

"It's okay if you don't want to talk about it."

Elena looked up at Mickey. "I'm glad you kill those men."

Mickey nodded and tightened her lips. *Me, too.*

***

The hours passed. The sky remained cloudless; the air hot. The wind remained constant and pushed the catamaran along at a good clip. The twin hulls cut through the water with very little motion. The boat rode flat on the surface.

Mickey and Elena chatted, made lunch together, ate at the saloon table near the cockpit, and chatted some more. Elena talked about her island, her family, and her school. Mickey talked about New York and her job.

Elena couldn't believe that one city could be bigger than her island of Maiao, or even the bigger island nearby. Given Elena's accent, Mickey didn't get the name of the bigger island until Elena had said it several times.

"The bigger island near your island is Tahiti?" Mickey asked.

"Yes. That island is near my home. Only one day away."

In the late afternoon, Mickey tossed the lure in the water and let the line play out. She secured the pole in the holder and made sure the clicker was engaged. She then went back to chatting with Elena. Twenty minutes later the Penn Senator reel squawked as the tip of the pole bent. Mickey kept the pole in the holder as she turned the crank. Her muscles flexed with each turn until the fish was only yards away from the stern.

Mickey motioned for Elena to grab the gaff hook and stand ready at the sugar scoop.

Elena took her position and waited for the fish to get closer.

Mickey struggled to turn the handle. She saw a flash of silver. *Could be a wahoo or tuna,* she thought.

Elena sent the gaff toward the fish and pulled up on what turned out to be a small wahoo. She grinned as she held the gaff up with the fish twisting and turning on the hook.

"You've done this before," Mickey yelled over the sound of the wind and water.

"Many times," Elena said. "I help my brother."

"Looks like we're having fish for dinner," Mickey said, as she relaxed her grip on the pole.

Elena lifted the fish to the cockpit floor, stepped on its tail, and removed the gaff.

Mickey retrieved a knife and a bucket from the galley and returned to the cockpit.

Elena reached for the knife and expertly began slicing the fish. Soon she had filets separated from the bones. She used the bucket to slosh water on the deck until the remains were washed overboard.

"Looks like you know what you're doing," Mickey said from behind the wheel as she watched Elena finish up with the fish.

Elena nodded. "This is very good fish."

"We can have the leftover rice, and maybe some papaya with it," Mickey said.

***

Mickey had already decided she would reef the main and jib sails at night, even if there were no storms evident. Squalls in the Pacific could come up quickly, according to Travis. Thomas had told her the same thing.

As the sun approached the horizon, Mickey turned her attention to the various lines running into the cockpit through the line clutches. Both Thomas and Travis had gone over this process with her several times. Travis highly suggested she reef the sail at night.

With the autopilot still engaged, to keep the boat on its heading, Mickey released the tension on the main sheet until the sail began to waffle in the wind. She then released the main halyard while maintaining its tension, and lowered the sail until it was at the first reefing point. She locked off the halyard and then pulled the two reefing lines to take up the slack. She placed tension on the reefing lines with the winch for the last bit. She locked the lines in the clutch block and then trimmed the main sheet until the reduced sail was taut against the wind.

Mickey climbed on top of the hard top to make sure all the extra sail was on the leeward side. She then returned to the cockpit and partially furled the jib.

She checked her heading, along with the wind direction and speed. The wind was still blowing at around twelve knots, but their speed had dropped to around four knots. Slower, but safer.

Elena once again watched Mickey go through the entire process. "How you learn to do this?"

"Some very good men taught me," Mickey said. She looked into Elena's eyes. "Not all men are bad. It's important that you know that."

"I know," Elena said. "Only some men."

Mickey nodded, smiled, and then turned to the sun sinking below the horizon.

CHAPTER 20

Without the sea sickness meds she had on Roundabout, Mickey felt a little queasy when below deck for extended periods. She therefore spent most of her time in the cockpit. That would be especially true at night, starting with the first night. She wanted to remain close to the helm so she could react to any alarms from the automatic identification system. Even though AIS was only good for those vessels with a transmitter, it was better than nothing.

With the limited ability to detect vessels always in the back of her mind, the boat's rocking and rolling, and the intermittent sail flapping, she found it nearly impossible to sleep.

For the umpteenth time, Mickey opened her eyes to find it still pitch dark. They had been out less than a full day and she was already exhausted.

She rose from the settee behind the saloon table and checked the chart plotter, which included the AIS information. The boat was alone and on track. Mickey was extremely pleased the autopilot functioned normally. Without it, she would be forced to heave-to in order to get some sleep. In that configuration the boat would continue generally in the right direction, but at a much slower pace. Over the course of the trip, it would add hours, if not days.

While she was up, she scanned the three hundred and sixty degrees of ocean around her for any boat navigation lights piercing the darkness. The only light she saw was the tiny glow at the top of the cat's own mast. Except for the chart plotter and the mast light, the boat was completely dark in order to conserve power.

She checked the battery indicator and found the needle pointing to a little less than eighty-five percent. That was good. As long as they had sunlight during the day and the wind spun the propeller driven turbine, the batteries would remain charged.

With all apparently secure, Mickey gazed at the dark lump on the starboard cockpit bench. Elena had a perfectly good bunk below, but insisted on remaining up top. About the only time she went below was to help Mickey in the galley, or to use the head.

That was another thing that pleased Mickey. Elena had caught on quickly to the head's operation, including the manual pump toilet. It involved flipping a lever, unlocking the handle, pumping up to twenty times, flipping the lever again, pump some more, and then lock the handle. It was a pain, but doable; certainly better than not having any bathroom. Mickey restricted use to just one of the two heads for both of them. If the toilet became clogged or stopped working, there was the other head for a backup.

Mickey thought it amazing how she now thought in terms of overlapping systems and backups. For some reason, given her exploits over the past few weeks, it had become important to always have a backup in case something broke. She never thought that way before. She just assumed things would work. And when they didn't, she called a repairman. But repairmen were few and far between on the open ocean. She suspected that just being around Thomas and Travis, both nautical in nature, had rubbed off. They both always seemed to be thinking about something. She found herself thinking about the little things a lot more, rather than just presuming everything would work out. She was proof-positive that sometimes, often maybe, things didn't work out.

Mickey scanned the ocean again, glanced at the chart plotter, and then padded her way back to the saloon. She reclined, closed her eyes, and tried to sleep.

***

A loud *bang* and a sudden more-than-normal roll to one side jolted Mickey from her snooze, sure she had only just closed her eyes. Disoriented, for a moment, she was back on board Roundabout just before it sank below the waves. Another *bang* and loud sail flapping brought her to full consciousness as she sat up.

Morning had brought increased winds and higher waves. The little boat dipped as it accepted a large spray of salt water across its bow.

Elena tried to sit up and was unceremoniously rolled to the deck. She wrestled with her blanket and grabbed a handful of the fiberglass locker she had been lying on. She pulled herself up on wobbly legs, as she tried to stand upright. She looked at Mickey. Confusion and fear etched across her face. "What is happening?" she yelled above the howl of the wind.

"A squall," Mickey yelled back. Hours of boredom, separated by moments of sheer terror. She couldn't remember who told her that about sailing, but it was certainly true.

Mickey made her way, handhold to handhold, to the helm. The autopilot was trying to keep the boat on course, but the wind had shifted to a broad reach and had increased to just under thirty-two knots. She scanned the dull gray of early morning and saw dark clouds in the distance.

Mickey turned to the lines clutch and immediately released tension on the main sail. She then went through the same process as before to put another reef in. There were only two reefing points, so this would be the last reef. Other than that, the only other option in high winds would be to drop the sail completely, and depend solely on a reduced jib. But she wanted to try the extra reef first.

She pulled on both reef lines and then used the winch for the last foot or so. Reefing line one pulled into position okay, but reefing line two appeared stuck. She was afraid to put more pressure on the winch, for fear of breaking the line or ripping the sail. As the wind increased, Mickey released the tension on the second reef line, climbed out of the cockpit, and up to the hardtop overhead.

The boat bucked up and down, side to side, as the wind increased. She should have taken the time to tie in to the life line that stretched from bow to stern on both sides, but she didn't. Then the rain came. Huge fat drops stung Mickey's exposed skin, mostly her face. She had to squint to keep from being hit in the eye from the lateral-flying water. The much colder rain brought goose pimples and a shiver to her skin.

She moved slowly and ensured her hands and feet had good purchase as she climbed and scooted across the fiberglass top. She grabbed the boom and pulled herself to a crouch as the wind buffeted the cold aluminum. The main sheets pulled tight, slackened, then tight again. The wind tried its best to swing the boom from one side to the other, but the preventer line Mickey had set kept it from swinging radically about.

With the rain and wind making it difficult to see, she inched her way to the mast and looked up with only a squint. She saw the problem immediately. Several feet up, one of the slides had wedged in the mast's track. If not resolved, the wind would either break the plastic slide or tear the sail. Mickey didn't want either of those things to happen, since she didn't have another sail and she didn't have any more slides.

She extended her hand, but found that the culprit was two feet out of reach, even when she stood on tiptoes. She could think of no other recourse but to climb up on the mast using the fold out footholds. In this wind, the last thing she wanted to do was climb the mast. She took two seconds to think about it and then unfolded the lowest foot hold. She stepped up, one hand around the mast, the other with a handful of sail gathered at the boom. She reached up, but was still a foot short. She released her handful of sail and unfolded the second foothold. She stepped up with the opposite foot, one hand still wrapped around the mast. High enough, she pounded her fist against the plastic slide, trying to force it back into the slot. As the boat bucked and the freezing rain pelted Mickey's face, the slide wouldn't budge. She tried again, but the slide would not move. She looked around at the bow as it dipped below a wave and then rose with a shower of spray. One trait she was sure she inherited from her father was a lack of patience. "You son of a bitch!" she yelled, as she slammed the bottom of her closed fist against the plastic. Two things happened. The slide popped back in place, and she fell backwards from the mast.

Looking straight up as she fell, her back and butt slammed into the hardtop. The flex cushioned most of the impact. Lying there, her t-shirt plastered against her body and her hair matted in tangles, she squinted up at the mast as it swung back and forth like the metronome she came to hate as a child. Her forced piano lessons flashed in her mind.

Her hand ached worse than her back, so she figured she probably didn't do any major damage to her spine. She took a deep breath to get her anger under control and then rolled to her hands and knees. She crawled to the edge, eased herself down, and flopped into the seat behind the wheel. She took several deep breaths as she massaged her hand and looked over at Elena.

Elena looked like she was on the back of a bucking bronco—both feet wide apart, knees bent with her thighs parallel to the deck, both hands wrapped knucklewhite around the edge of the opening to the saloon. The boat bucked again and Elena rode it through. She stared with her mouth agape; eyes wide and locked on Mickey.

"We're okay," Mickey said. "I'm okay. The boat's okay. You're okay." She heard herself say the words, but even she was not sure they were true. She then turned her attention back to the lines. She cranked the winch until the second reef line pulled into position. She locked the reef line in the clutch and then went through the process to reduce the jib until it was only a small white triangle against a black sky.

After trimming both sails, she checked the speed indicator. The digits indicated nine knots. *Never let a good storm go to waste*, she thought, as she adjusted the heading, reset the autopilot, and watched the speed over ground edge up to twelve knots. And then fifteen knots. She wanted to take advantage of the speed, even if the heading was slightly off.

Despite shivering from the cold, she hesitated to go below for a towel. Two reasons. She didn't want to get banged around down there, and she knew it would only take seconds for seasickness to hit. She continued to shiver as she watched the instruments, the sails, and the boat as it pounded through the waves. All she could do at this point was hold tight, ride out the storm, and hope the sails didn't rip.

She kept an eye on the main and wondered whether she should lower it completely. She watched as the wind whipped the cloth bunched at the boom. She wished Travis or Thomas was here, but they weren't. It was up to her. And she flatly did not know what to do.

At that moment, the boat began surfing down the side of a deep trough. Mickey watched as the boat seemed to drop almost vertically toward the dark ocean below. When it reached the bottom, the bow of both hulls buried themselves into the opposite side of the steep wall of water. The building mass then rolled over the bows, right up to the cockpit windows. The tons of excess water then poured off the sides and the front of the boat popped back to the surface, prepared to do it all again.

Mickey looked over at Elena and found her prone on the deck, arms stretched above her head, hands wrapped around the edge of the saloon opening. Her eyes and mouth were contorted into lines of absolute terror. She cried out. Mickey didn't understand the words, but she got the idea. Mickey wasn't far behind.

Suddenly the boat jerked and Elena's body slid across the deck with the slosh of several inches of sea water trapped in the cockpit. Then the boat twisted, sending Elena's body back against the locker. Her hip slammed into the fiberglass and she lost her grip on the saloon opening. She then slid into the saloon, and immediately back out to the cockpit. She slammed against the transom. Water washed over the gunwales and for a moment, Elena disappeared beneath the white foam.

Mickey yelled for Elena to grab hold of something, as she looked toward the open port and starboard hatches in the saloon, both leading down below. Mickey would have no clue as to what she would do if both hulls became swamped with water. The boat probably wouldn't sink, but it also wouldn't be floating the way a boat is supposed to float. She had to do something.

She glanced at Elena and saw that she was holding onto the guardrail with both hands, apparently secure for the moment. Mickey then glanced at her left hand, wrapped over the top of the deck winch, and at her right hand curled around the edge of the saloon opening. Reluctant to let go with either hand, she looked at the several inches of water gathered in the cockpit and saloon, and watched it begin to slosh over the raised bottom edges of the hatch openings. Water would be pouring into the galley on the starboard side, and into the cabins on the port side, if she didn't get the hatch covers placed.

She took a deep breath, released her grip with both hands, and then launched herself toward the starboard hatch. She plunged into the accumulated water, blinked to clear her vision, and then latched onto the bottom edge of the hatch.

As her body sloshed back and forth, she tried to remember the location of the separate clear plastic hatch covers. Then she remembered they were both wedged in a cubbyhole in the galley.

Mickey wrapped both hands around the vertical edges of the hatch and pulled herself up to the opening. She twisted her body around and slid both feet under her butt and then pulled herself to a crouch. She put one foot through the hatch opening and down to the first step.

At that moment the boat vaulted, tossing her to the galley deck below. She slammed to the already soaked floor, her head just missing the edge of the countertop along the starboard bulkhead. She took a second to ensure nothing was broken and then slid herself along the deck to the hatch covers. She pulled them out and wedged both under her left arm.

With the tiny room bucking back and forth, slamming her against the various appliances and surfaces, she slowly made her way back to the ladder.

She climbed the slippery steps to the top and then leapt to the saloon deck above. The hatch covers slipped from her hold and plunged into the water covering the deck.

With the covers threatening to slosh out of reach, she grabbed one, worked it into the slotted sides of the hatch opening, and then slammed the cover into position.

With the motion of the boat, she let her body slide to the other side of the saloon, toward the port hatch, scooping up the second hatch cover on the way. With much effort and a little finesse, the port cover slammed into place.

Mickey then turned her body around while in a sitting position, wrapped both hands around the saloon table pedestal, and looked back at Elena.

She was still holding tight to the guardrail. Her hair draped over her face in a wet, matted mass of tangled strands. Her eyes were closed, and she appeared to be praying.

Over the next couple of hours the storm lessened, until by midday the wind had subsided and the rain had dwindled to a light drizzle.

With the boat still being jostled by the waves, Mickey pushed herself with sore muscles to a standing position.

Most of the water in the cockpit and saloon had worked its way out of the drains, but the boat was still soggy with moisture throughout. The boat needed to be washed down with fresh water, but she didn't have the water to spare. Plus, she was totally spent. Alive, with nothing broken, but spent. With no sleep the previous night, and the extreme exertion of dealing with the storm, the only thing Mickey wanted to do was collapse on the cushioned bench behind the saloon table. With limp noodles for legs, she ambled over and plopped down. She tucked her knees up and closed her eyes with a renewed appreciation for those guys who solo sail the open ocean. She opened her eyes long enough to see that Elena was stretched out on the cockpit bench and then closed them again.

By mid afternoon her stomach, reminding her she hadn't eaten, forced her to rise. With bruised and sore legs, arms, and back she limped to the helm, checked the instruments, and reset the autopilot. She was amazed it still worked.

She rousted Elena and they set about putting the boat back the way it was before the storm.

A late lunch consisted of fish salad on crackers, made from the leftover fish from the night before and some pickle relish and mayonnaise from the cruiser.

Late afternoon brought an end to the drizzle and a bit of sun. The wind turned to the starboard beam at around 15 knots.

Mickey hoisted both sails, reset the course and autopilot, and relaxed as she scanned the open water, despite her still-heavy eyelids. She glanced at Elena, who was back curled up on the opposite bench.

Mickey was well aware she would not make it through another sleepless night, so she took a look around the open ocean, checked the AIS, and then reclined on the port cockpit bench. The boat's gentle rocking had her asleep in less than a minute.

***

An aroma brought her back to consciousness. Something smelled good. Mickey opened her eyes, raised her head, and looked around. She saw Elena sitting at the saloon table, eating something from a bowl.

Mickey rose, massaged her sore back, and then stood. She checked the horizon and then checked Elena's bowl. "Looks like chicken noodle."

Elena paused with her spoon in mid air. "I don't know. Can't read words on the top. Good though." She slurped the soup from the spoon.

Knowing what's in the can would be a problem for Elena, since all the labels were removed. Susan did the same thing with the cans on Roundabout. She said it had to do with the moisture and the labels not sticking. So they went ahead and removed the labels and wrote the name of the contents on the top with a Sharpie. That meant there were no pictures of the contents. And even if Elena could read English, she probably couldn't read the hen scratching of whoever wrote the name of the contents. Elena was lucky she didn't open a can of butter beans.

Mickey checked the sails, which were still reduced, and then the horizon. She had slept most of the day while the boat ran with sails reefed. That meant they had lost out on some distance. The sleep was worth it though. Since there were still several hours until dark, Mickey decided to raise the sails. She worked the lines until the main was at the top of the mast and then unfurled the jib. Without looking at the speed indicator, she could feel the boat's acceleration.

Mickey went below, heated up a can of vegetable beef, and returned to the saloon table. She glanced at Elena's empty bowl. "Still hungry? Mickey asked. "Get whatever you want. More soup. Or there's cheese and crackers down there. Cheese is in the fridge."

Elena left and then returned a couple of minutes later with a block of cheddar, a box of wheat crackers, and a knife.

Mickey opened the cheese and then sliced thin squares. She placed one on a cracker and popped it in her mouth. She motioned with her chin. "You'll like it," she mumbled with her mouth full.

Elena repeated the process, chewed, and swallowed. She nodded and then cut another piece.

"Do you have cheese on your island?"

"Sometimes," she said.

Mickey was finding it hard to find something to talk about. She and Elena had zero common experiences, and Elena was generally not that talkative. Mickey didn't want to make her uncomfortable by asking a lot of questions, especially about her time on the cruiser. It was pretty clear what she had gone through. Reliving it wouldn't help. And she didn't seem all that interested in where Mickey came from or her work. Elena wouldn't understand anything about advertising and it would be pointless to try to explain it. The only thing they had in common was the boat they both occupied.

They spent the rest of the afternoon trying to remove the moisture from below deck. They fully opened the saloon hatches to both hulls. Unfortunately, there were no other portholes or hatches below deck to be opened, which meant there wasn't any cross breeze below deck. With the heat and the moisture, both hulls turned into saunas. The master cabin did include a small fan mounted to the bulkhead. Using it would burn power, but Mickey thought it would be okay, especially during the day with the bright sun sending rays to the solar panels. She flipped the fan on and let it run. There wasn't much she could do about the galley side of the boat, except try to remove any excess water.

They used towels to sop up as much of the water as possible below deck. It didn't really help the moisture problem much and soon both Mickey and Elena were dripping with sweat.

When they had removed as much water as possible, Mickey dropped her towel in the half-filled bucket, and wiped sweat from her forehead with the back of her hand. "That's about all we can do," she said.

Elena dropped her towel in the bucket and got to her feet. Her t-shirt was completely soaked and stuck to her skin. She pushed a strand of wet hair from her face.

"It will be night soon," Mickey said. "I say we reduce the sails early, heave to, and go for a short swim."

Elena cocked her head back and forth and then nodded.

Mickey went up to the cockpit, released the necessary line clutches, and then put one reef in the main. She then released the sheet lines and let both sails go limp.

The boat slowed to a crawl, and then came to an almost complete stop.

Mickey peeled off her clothes and jumped in the water from the starboard sugar scoop. She was in for only a few seconds and then pulled herself out and back to the top of the sugar scoop. She then rinsed her clothes in the ocean, wrung them out, and draped them over the guardrail.

While Elena repeated the process, Mickey went below and then returned with a bucket of fresh water. "I think we've earned a fresh water rinse," she said to Elena as she crawled out of the water. Mickey used a mug and slowly poured the fresh water over Elena's head until most of the salt water was washed away, and then did the same for her own body. With the bucket still half full of fresh water, she rinsed her shorts and top. She did the same with Elena's clothes and then draped everything back over the guardrail.

They both then toweled off, wrapped themselves in the towels, and moved back to the cockpit.

Mickey gathered the dirty bowls, cheese, and crackers still on the saloon table, and deposited them in the galley, where she washed and put the bowls away. She then joined Elena back in the cockpit.

Mickey thought about how she had jumped in the ocean, leaving Elena on the boat alone and imagined being separated from the boat by the current or wind. Would Elena know how to turn the boat? She motioned Elena over to the helm and pointed to the lines running through the block. She went through an explanation of each line, where it led, and what it did. She explained the winch and that she should be very careful with the winch handle. There were only two on board. Mickey remembered the navy seals quote which Thomas had repeated a hundred times. *Two is one, and one is none.*

A few weeks earlier, Mickey knew nothing about a sailboat. Now, she was the expert between the two of them. She was an expert only if nothing serious went wrong. Mickey would have no clue what to do if a sail ripped, or if the furling line to the jib broke. Even with Mickey's limited experience, she knew both were common occurrences on a sailboat on the open ocean, based on conversations with Thomas and Travis.

Elena seemed to have the general idea, so Mickey walked her through the process, starting with letting the tension off the sheets. She seemed interested in learning how it all worked. Even if she did nothing the whole voyage, and said nothing, Mickey was happy to have her on board. She wasn't happy about how she came to be on board, but her company was appreciated.

With the sails reefed and trimmed, the chart plotter, AIS, and autopilot checked and double checked, Mickey relaxed behind the wheel and watched as the last of the sun slid behind the horizon. The low clouds reflected shades and shapes of deep orange. Soon the light faded and everything beyond the cockpit transformed to black.

CHAPTER 21

With the morning sky still overcast, Mickey stared at a speck on the horizon.

Elena joined her and peered in the same direction. "A boat."

Mickey nodded. "Looks like a container ship. Heading west." She thought about trying to raise the ship on VHF, but decided against it. Even if the ship responded to her mayday, the captain would never alter course in order to deliver Mickey and Elena to Hawaii. He would push on to his destination. Mickey did not want to end up in Shanghai. So she watched as the speck disappeared.

She turned her attention to the chart plotter and adjusted the screen. The triangle representing their boat was a little less than a third of the way to Hawaii. They had made good progress, so far.

She checked the battery indicator. The needle hovered at seventy-eight percent. Not that bad, considering the lack of sunlight. The wind turbine was definitely helping. But just the same, Mickey hoped for more sun. She also hoped for more wind.

She looked around at the flat ocean and then to the wind speed indicator. The digits read six knots; the boat was ambling along at barely two knots. If this kept up, they would definitely be adding time to their trip.

***

Just after lunch, the wind speed dropped to near zero. The main, jib, and the boat sat motionless. Despite very little sun, the air was stifling.

Mickey and Elena lounged in the saloon. They both glistened with sweat.

Mickey wiped at her eyebrow. "This is one of the bad things about being on a boat," she said, "moisture and salt. Together they make everything sticky."

Elena nodded as she sat there with her eyes closed. Head back. "Is it hot in New York?"

"Sometimes. But it also gets very cold. People have to wear heavy coats there in certain months."

Suddenly, Mickey heard the main sail waffle lightly. She stood and stepped to the transom. She felt a puff of air. And then another. "I think the wind might be coming up."

Elena joined her. "I feel it."

The main sail tightened against the sheets and then took on more of a concave appearance. The boat wobbled.

Mickey checked the wind speed. "Up to six knots, and we're moving. Two knots. Four knots." Mickey looked at Elena and smiled. "I think we have our wind back."

Over the next few hours, the wind grew until it reached a steady fourteen knots. The cloud cover cleared and the trickle from the solar panels increased.

While the ocean was relatively calm, Mickey and Elena went below and cleaned up the galley. Just as they climbed the ladder and stepped into the saloon, the VHF squawked. "Ahoy, catamaran," came a man's voice.

Mickey jumped at the sudden intrusion. A man's voice was the last thing she expected. She immediately scanned her surroundings and saw sails in the distance, off the starboard bow.

She wasn't sure what she should do. Thomas always acknowledged callers. But Mickey and Elena were two women, alone. Still, it was difficult to pretend they weren't there.

Mickey picked up the handset and keyed the mic. "Ahoy, monohull." They exchanged pleasantries for a couple of minutes, which was common courtesy for yachts on the open ocean. Mickey saw no point in mentioning her situation, and the events on Palmyra. She might have if the captain intended to stop at Palmyra, but he didn't. His voyage had taken him from California to Hawaii, and now he was on to Sydney. He was traveling in pretty much the opposite direction. Two ships passing in the night; actually, day in this case. Chances were pretty good he had a satellite phone and probably a single sideband radio capable of reaching Hawaii, but Mickey was making progress. There was no reason to involve anyone else at this point.

It was just as well. With little food, and even fewer clothes, Mickey wasn't in the mood to entertain guests. She bid the captain a good voyage and signed off.

Elena stood close by, obviously intrigued by the back and forth on the radio. She probably wondered why Mickey didn't ask for help. But Elena didn't say anything.

Mickey took that as a good sign. Elena apparently trusted that Mickey could sail the boat to its destination. *Confidence begets confidence*, Mickey thought.

***

By the fourth day Mickey and Elena had fallen into a routine. Mickey dozed a lot of the daylight hours, confident that Elena would wake her if anything didn't seem right. Elena was okay at reading the chart plotter and the AIS. Plus, an alarm would sound if the AIS picked up a boat that might cross their course.

Elena prepared most of the meals, kept the boat tidy, and then slept most of the night hours.

Day or night, Mickey never really got enough sleep at any one time. She was always in that light sleep arena, in which the least little noise would bring her to consciousness. It was one of those times when Mickey was somewhere between totally awake and a deep sleep when she heard a loud splash and then a snort. She opened her eyes and immediately saw Elena gazing at something off the port side. The morning air was still cooler than it would be later and the sky was mostly cloudless. "What is it?" Mickey asked as she stretched and got to her feet.

"Whale," Elena said, as she pointed in the distance.

Just as Mickey looked in that direction, she saw a geyser of water. Then a large flipper broke the surface and slowly sank out of sight. Mickey had seen a whale on the trip with Thomas and Susan, but this one was much closer. And scarier. Mickey felt sure the whale was no threat to them, but still, the boat was tiny compared to the whale. An accidental flip of its tail against the hulls would easily toss the boat over.

They watched the whale break the surface and then dip below several more times as it moved off into the distance. Mickey thought about how fleeting and how random life could be. She thought about how she had survived, and how Thomas and Susan had not. It could just as easily have gone the other way. She wondered whether life truly had a design, or was it all just a jumble of arbitrary events where some lived and others didn't.

She scanned the ocean once again and then returned to her perch. She watched Elena move about the deck, felt the gentle breeze, and the absence of rocking as the boat took on the nearly flat sea.

***

The morning of day five started like most of the others. The ocean was mostly flat, the wind was moderate, and the clouds were light.

Elena stirred from the bench in the saloon when Mickey started tugging on the lines to raise the main and jib sails. At their full glory, the sails caught the wind and pulled the little boat along at an increasing clip. The boat topped out at around eight knots, a very satisfactory speed.

Mickey tossed the lure in the water, let some line play out from the Penn Senator reel, and then made sure the rod was secure in the holder at the stern. She then went below to the head, and then to the galley, where Elena was already sifting through cans for something for breakfast.

"How about some oatmeal?" Mickey asked, as she joined Elena at the counter.

Elena nodded and then together they went about preparing two bowls of hot porridge, topped with a few raisins and some cinnamon.

As they stepped out to the saloon carrying the steaming bowls, Mickey caught sight of movement off the starboard bow. A boat.

She sat her bowl down on the saloon table and then moved to the bow where she peered at the fast moving boat, well over four or five miles out. It was a large cabin cruiser, bow riding high. No sign of any people. Still, Mickey had a bad feeling.

Elena, standing beside her, looked into Mickey's eyes. Fear crept into the lines on her forehead. She didn't say anything as she looked back at the boat.

The cruiser had to remind her of the Darrel and Raphael situation that ended only days earlier. She obviously feared a repeat.

Mickey patted Elena on the shoulder and then shuffled back to the helm. She checked the course and speed, the sails, to make sure they were trimmed as well as possible given the fourteen knot wind, and then the chart plotter. The cruiser did not appear on the AIS, which either meant the boat didn't have an AIS transmitter, or it was turned off.

Mickey went below to the master cabin and retrieved the pistol she lifted from Darrel's boat. Might as well have the gun handy. She then returned to the cockpit. The cruiser, two or three miles out, was still on course to intercept the cat.

Mickey placed the pistol under the cushion of the helm seat and then returned to the saloon table. "Elena," she called out. "Let's finish our breakfast."

CHAPTER 22

The cruiser passed the cat's starboard side at full speed and continued on.

Mickey exhaled a sigh of relief, but then tensed when she heard the rev of the cruiser's engine drop a couple of octaves. She watched the boat slow, make a sharp turn well off the cat's stern, and then pull up along the cat's starboard.

Mickey stood at the helm and watched for any people to appear.

After a few moments a woman in her mid-forties, wearing white shorts and a bikini top, stepped into view and waved.

Mickey picked up the VHF radio handset and keyed the mike. "Cruiser pacing the catamaran, what can we do for you?"

For several seconds there was only static while the woman ducked inside. A few moments later, a female voice came over the radio. "We have…"

The transmission broke off after the two words, as though the sender had let off the mic key.

"We have a bit of an emergency," the female voice finally said.

Mickey shook her head. Whatever was going on over there, it didn't look right or feel right. Mickey rubbed her face, not sure what to do. It could be an actual emergency. Even if it was, Mickey wasn't sure what she could do. Or it could be a ruse to get Mickey to stop. Mickey had no intention of slowing her vessel, not without a lot more information.

She glanced at Elena, who stood to Mickey's side. Her face made it clear what she was thinking.

Finally, Mickey keyed the mic. "What sort of emergency?"

There was a long pause before the female voice came back. "We have an injured person over here."

"What sort of injury?" Mickey asked. She waited several seconds for a response, but there was only dead air. Mickey let out a long exhale. "I repeat, what sort of injury?"

Suddenly the cruiser increased its speed and veered toward the cat until there were only a few feet between the two boats.

Mickey flipped the autopilot off and turned the wheel to port as she keyed the mic. "What are you doing?" she yelled.

The cruiser swerved back to the right, increasing the distance between them, and slowed.

Mickey's hands began to shake and her knees became weak. She took a deep breath. *Panic won't help the situation.* She was fully aware that the much bigger and heavier cruiser could crush the cat, without doing a lot of damage to its own hull. There was no way to outrun the motor boat. If it wanted to do harm, it easily could, and there was nothing Mickey could really do to stop it. She keyed the mic again and tried to keep the fear from her voice. "What do you want?"

"I want you to stop," a man's voice said over the radio.

At this point, Elena shook almost uncontrollably as she held onto the edge of the saloon opening. Tears ran down both cheeks as she glanced at Mickey.

Mickey felt like crying as well, but someone had to hold it together. She gave Elena a reassuring nod and then keyed the mic. "I have no intention of stopping."

A few seconds later the cruiser once again accelerated and veered sharply toward the cat. At the last possible moment, the motor boat cut back.

"I said, stop your boat," said the man's voice, "or I'll stop it for you."

So far Mickey had seen only the woman and heard transmissions from a woman and a man. Two people. There might be only two people on board, but somehow Mickey doubted that. And she still didn't know what they wanted. What could two or more people on a large cruiser possibly want from a small sailboat, which wasn't large enough to house a lot of possessions? Maybe they wanted money. Or maybe they wanted Mickey and Elena.

Mickey stared at Elena for several long moments. The shaking was uncontrollable, and she looked like she was about to collapse. Mickey felt pretty much the same, she just hid it better. Mickey considered the situation and decided she had no real choice. She believed the man would ram the sailboat if Mickey didn't comply. At least by stopping, they might have a chance.

Mickey released the lines and let the sails swing to a neutral position. They fluttered in the moderate breeze over the largely flat ocean as Mickey let the boat slowly come to a complete stop.

Elena slid her butt down along the edge of the saloon opening to the deck and wept.

Mickey knelt and placed a hand on her shoulder. She lifted Elena's chin. Mickey raised an eyebrow. "Trust me with this," she said. "Everything will be okay." She nodded and then stood to face the cruiser which had slowed and was maneuvering alongside.

Mickey wasn't sure if everything would be okay, but she intended to do everything possible to make it that way. She thought of the pistol under the cushion, only a couple of feet away. She ran through her mind how to hold the gun. She thought of all the movies she had seen in which the scared woman pointed the gun at the approaching stranger until he slowly took the gun from the woman's hand. Mickey made up her mind that she wouldn't let that happen. She would shoot if necessary. Without hesitation.

As the cruiser drifted up to the cat, two men emerged from the wheel house. One held the woman Mickey saw earlier. The man's fingers pressed into the woman's upper arm. She looked just as scared as Mickey felt.

"I'm sorry," the woman said. "They have my husband and children."

Mickey knew there were pirates in the oceans. Hijacking off the African coast, and even parts of South America, were well publicized. But given the number of private yachts cruising the world, the chances of actually running into a pirate situation was actually rare. At least according to Thomas. He and Susan had cruised numerous times without a problem. Mickey, on the other hand, had apparently run into pirates twice in a matter of days. Bad luck, or was it destiny?

The man visibly tightened his grip on the woman's arm until she winced with pain. Her knees buckled as her chin dipped and she began to cry.

"What do you want?" Mickey asked. At this point, Mickey had seen no weapons. Just the two men. But both were large, grimy looking, as though they hadn't showered in weeks. One of the men wore a button-down shirt left unbuttoned, exposing his protruding stomach. The other man at least buttoned his shirt, but he looked just as mean.

The man with the buttoned shirt smiled without saying anything as he reached out for the cat's guard rail and pulled the two boats closer together. He then stepped into the cockpit next to Mickey. His odor was overpowering. He glanced at Elena crumpled on the deck. His smile grew larger.

"See what's below," the man still on the cruiser said. He released his grasp on the woman's arm as he shoved her to a sitting position on a locker at the transom. She shook her head and took a deep breath, obviously weary of the ordeal.

The man on the cat disappeared down the cat's port ladder.

"Are your husband and children still alive?" Mickey asked the woman.

The woman nodded. "Tied up below," she said.

"Just the two men?" Mickey asked.

The woman started to answer, but then abruptly stopped when the man shot her a look. She slumped and cowered. When the man looked back at Mickey, the woman raised her eyes to Mickey and nodded with a subtle dip of her chin.

Two men. Mickey needed to get them together. Mickey doubted she could shoot the man on the cat when he came back up and shoot the man on the cruiser. With both boats moving, she doubted she could hit anything much over a couple of feet. Especially with the pistol and its short barrel. But getting them together and close, with Mickey in possession of the pistol, would likely be a problem. Wearing her tight shorts and top, there was no place to hide the gun on her person. It was clear that Mickey had to find a way to get them both on the cat. If they took her to the cruiser she would have no chance.

The man who had gone below on the cat came up from the port side and then down into the galley on the starboard side.

Mickey knew the only thing they would find of value on the boat was already in sight: Mickey and Elena. When the man in the galley came back up with nothing, Mickey's time would be up. They would force the two girls to the cruiser and that would be that.

With that scenario in mind, Mickey leaned back against the helm seat as nonchalantly as possible. She kept her eyes on the man standing in the back of the cruiser and waited for an opportunity.

When the man glanced into the cruiser's wheelhouse, Mickey took that split second to slip her hand under the seat's cushion and retrieve the pistol. She held it in her hand behind her, out of sight when the man turned his attention back to her. With him watching, Mickey slowly stood, let her gun hand drop to her right buttock, and took the three steps over to Elena, still on the deck crying. Mickey knelt behind her in a consoling manner and placed her free hand on her shoulder.

"Do you trust me?" Mickey whispered into Elena's ear.

Elena nodded slightly while sobbing. Tears poured down her cheek.

Mickey continued to whisper. "I'm going to slide something into your waist band, behind your back, and cover it with your shirt. It's a gun. Don't touch it. Act like it's not there. They are going to take us to the cruiser."

Elena sobbed more.

"Listen to me," Mickey said. "They are going to take us to the cruiser. Make sure you stay close to me. When the time is right, I'll get the gun."

Elena wiped her cheeks with her hands and looked up at Mickey.

Mickey squeezed her lips together and lifted her chin slightly.

Elena nodded as she looked back down at the deck.

The man on the boat kept his eyes on Mickey and Elena with renewed interest. "Dominick, what the hell's keeping you?" he yelled.

Mickey heard footsteps heading back to the ladder, which meant she had only a few seconds. She slid her left hand from Elena's shoulder, down her back, as though consoling her. She lifted the back of Elena's t-shirt, used her fingers to separate the waist band from her skin, and then slid the pistol inside the waist band. Mickey smoothed Elena's t-shirt over the pistol just as the man below stepped to the saloon deck.

"They have nothing," the man yelled.

"Bring the two girls," the man on the cruiser yelled.

The man on the cat reached down and grabbed Elena's arm and began pulling her to her feet.

Elena screamed and pulled back.

Mickey placed one hand on Elena's shoulder and the other on the man's arm. "I'll do it."

The man released his grasp and stepped back. He lifted both palms in a gesture to go ahead.

Standing behind Elena, Mickey grasped both her upper arms and gently encouraged her to her feet.

"Just stay with me," Mickey said to Elena as Elena slowly rose to her feet.

The man on the cat ushered the two girls along with an extended hand, but he remained a couple of steps back.

Mickey stayed behind Elena as they both shuffled to the gunwale.

When the man on the cruiser stepped forward to help Elena across, Mickey suddenly pulled the pistol from Elena's waist band, spun around, pointed, and pulled the trigger twice.

The deafening blasts sent both rounds into the chest of the man behind her, knocking him backwards.

Mickey immediately spun around and pointed the gun at the man on the cruiser.

The man on the cruiser raised his hands slowly. "Hold up there, missy," the man said. "We meant no harm."

Mickey let the barrel dip as she blinked one time, very slowly. "I'm getting real tired of men who mean me no harm." She raised the barrel and fired two more rounds, point blank.

Both rounds sent the man backwards until he stumbled and fell to the deck.

The woman, still sitting at the transom, screamed, and then brought her hand to her open mouth.

Mickey looked down at Elena, who was crumpled on the deck next to the gunwale. Her eyes were wide as they stared up at Mickey. Mickey walked over to the man lying flat on the cat's cockpit deck.

Blood began to spread across the fabric of the man's shirt. He took two more breaths before his chest sunk, lifeless, and his chin flopped to one side.

Mickey looked back at the man on the cruiser.

He, too, appeared lifeless.

Mickey took a deep breath as her shaking hand dropped the pistol to the deck. She slumped to both knees and dropped her chin to her chest. She closed her eyes and took several more deep breaths.

CHAPTER 23

Mickey composed herself and then scooted over to Elena, who was still scrunched in a corner of the cockpit. "Are you okay?" she asked, as she placed a hand on Elena's leg.

Elena looked up and nodded with a gentle dip of her chin.

"How about if we move you over to the saloon," Mickey said, as she placed a hand under Elena's arm.

They both rose up and Mickey guided Elena to the bench behind the saloon table.

"I'll be right back," Mickey said, as she turned her attention to the cruiser.

The woman still sat, sobbing at the stern.

Mickey lashed the two boats together with a piece of rope, then hopped over the gunwale of both boats, and landed on the cruiser's deck. She went to the woman and touched her shoulder. "You alright?"

The woman wiped her cheek and looked up at Mickey. She started to say something, but then turned her gaze to the dead man lying on the deck.

"What is your name?" Mickey asked.

"Charlotte," the woman said.

Mickey gave a weak smile. "Let's go check on your husband and kids."

The woman nodded and then got to her feet. She led the way into the wheelhouse and then down a ladder. She opened one of the cabin doors and then rushed to a man, also in his forties, who was tied and gagged. She pulled the gag from his mouth.

"What the hell happened up there?" the man asked.

Charlotte started explaining as Mickey stepped forward and helped untie the man's feet and hands.

Mickey then turned to the two kids, a boy and a girl, both early-to-mid teens, and began untying them. "My name is Mickey. The two men tried to hijack my boat."

"Where are they?" the man asked, as he slipped the last of his restraints from his wrists and stood up.

The woman glanced at Mickey.

"They're both up on deck," Mickey said. "And they're both dead."

The man stared at Mickey for several long moments, glanced at his wife and kids, and then rushed from the room.

Mickey followed him up to the stern and watched as he knelt beside the dead man.

"You did this?" he asked.

"Didn't have a choice," Mickey said.

The man rubbed the whiskers on his chin as he gazed over at the cat. He stepped closer to the gunwale for a better look at the second dead man. He then looked back at Mickey. "I don't believe in violence, and I certainly don't condone the use of guns. Did you have to kill them?"

"Would you rather they kill you and rape your wife and kids?"

The man rubbed his chin again and then, almost imperceptibly, shook his head side to side. He glanced at both men again and then at his wife and kids, who emerged from the wheelhouse. He looked back at Mickey. "Now what?"

Charlotte stepped closer. "Now we dump their bodies in the ocean."

The man stared at his wife.

"What happened?" Mickey asked. "How did they get control of your boat?"

The man took a deep breath and then sat on the locker at the stern. "I'm Steve, by the way. This is my wife Charlotte, daughter Melody, and son Chet." He motioned toward each one. "And you said your name is Mickey?"

"Yes," Mickey said. "Tell me what happened."

Steve stood and then paced back and forth. "In route to Maui, we took shelter in Hilo to wait out some bad weather. We took the opportunity to restock some of our provisions and left the boat for a few hours. When we returned, the weather was good enough to proceed, so we shoved off. We didn't know we had stowaways until we were at sea. They showed themselves, overpowered me, and took over the boat. They locked us below." He looked at his wife. "That was three days ago, I think, when we left Hilo." He looked at Charlotte.

Charlotte nodded.

"I don't know what their intentions were," Steve said. "They tied and gagged the kids and me, apparently when they saw your boat."

Mickey peered at the two kids.

They both sat shivering, even though the sun was bright and the air hot.

"Given that they tied you up below and terrorized your wife and kids, I'd say their intentions were obvious," Mickey said. "They were probably trying to figure out what to do with you."

Steve went to the bloody man on the deck and checked his pockets. He stood up. "Nothing. No ID."

"I don't want to know who they are," Charlotte said. "I just want them off my boat."

Mickey took a seat on a locker, raised her eyes to the sky for a few moments, and then back to Steve. "I only see two options. Continue to Hawaii with the men and report the matter to the authorities."

"Or?" Steve asked, as he kept his eyes on Mickey.

"Dump them in the ocean," Charlotte said.

Mickey nodded.

"I think we need to report the matter," Steve said. "Two men are dead." He motioned to his family. "And we didn't kill them."

"Look," Mickey said, as she gazed at Charlotte, the kids, and Steve in turn, "I felt threatened. I had every right to defend myself. Their intentions were obvious to me. And I had no interest in becoming one of their captives." Mickey locked her gaze on Charlotte. "Did they harm you in any way?"

Steve looked at his wife.

Charlotte glanced at the kids and then at Steve. "The fat one was pretty free with his hands. And he glared at Melody. A lot."

Steve stomped over to his wife. "Did he—?"

"No," Charlotte said. "But he would have, eventually."

Steve raised his head and stared out at the ocean. He rubbed his chin and then the back of his neck. He then turned to Mickey. "It's legal to defend yourself, but it's illegal to let this go unreported."

Charlotte went to the dead man and tried to lift him over the gunwale. "He's not staying on my boat," she said, as she huffed and grunted.

Mickey glanced at Steve, who stood frozen in the middle of the deck. She then joined Charlotte and helped slide the dead man up and over the gunwale.

The man splashed into the ocean, floated for a moment, and then slowly sank.

"There's another one over here," Mickey said, as she stepped off toward the cat.

Charlotte joined her and together they heaved and pushed the other man over the side.

He floated longer, but then eventually sank.

Mickey remained on the cat while Charlotte hopped back to the cruiser.

Charlotte shook Steve by the shoulders. "Get the boat going," she said, as she untied the rope holding the two boats together. "I believe we were headed for Maui." Charlotte then turned to Mickey. "Thank you. I have no doubt we would have ended up dead without your help."

Mickey nodded. "Good luck."

Charlotte then turned back to Steve. "Get the boat going," she said, as she pushed him toward the wheelhouse. She followed him with a final wave at Mickey.

Mickey watched Steve and Charlotte disappear into the wheelhouse. A few seconds later the engine started, and the boat slowly pulled away.

Melody and Chet gave a slight wave at Mickey as the two boats separated.

Mickey waved back and then watched the boat accelerate. Soon the boat was a tiny dot on the horizon.

Mickey retrieved a bucket, filled it with sea water several times, and sloshed the dead man's blood from the deck. She then scrubbed the spot and sloshed more water. Finished, she turned to Elena, still at the saloon table. She was keeled over, asleep on the bench cushions.

***

The next morning, day six of their voyage, brought overcast skies and a light breeze. The wind picked up by midmorning, and then a steady rain, with moderate winds by noon.

Mickey gathered as much rain water as possible for the boat's water tank, and she and Elena both took the opportunity to wash their bodies, hair, and clothes with fresh water. Wrapped in towels, they tied their clothes to the guardrail and let them flap in the wind.

By late afternoon the rain cleared, the clouds opened up, and the sun came out.

With steady winds and the boat on course, both Mickey and Elena caught up on lost sleep for a few hours. Mickey took the bench behind the saloon table. On one of those rare occasions, Elena went below to sleep.

Such was pretty much the routine over the following days. Mickey concentrated on keeping the sails trimmed and the boat on course. Elena actually reeled in a Mahi and a small tuna.

Mickey and Elena talked at length about happy times in their lives. Mickey described New York and offered to host Elena, should she ever want to visit. Mickey promised to visit Elena's island, but it probably would not be right away.

Two days after the incident with the two men, Mickey got Elena laughing again. At that point, all signs of fear and anxiety were gone finally, and Elena spent less time sleeping and more time helping out with the boat. She became pretty good at managing the lines and keeping the boat on course.

Mid-afternoon of the tenth day, Mickey spotted the island of Oahu poking just above the horizon. She checked the distance and speed over ground on the plot charter and determined that if the wind continued, they would arrive well after nightfall. Mickey reduced the sails early to slow their progress so they would pull into the Honolulu harbor the next morning.

Early on the eleventh day Mickey contacted the Honolulu harbor master via VHF to alert him of their arrival and arrange for a spot to dock the boat. She also asked that the authorities be notified to meet the boat. Mickey wanted to report the loss of her sister, and the incident on Palmyra, as soon as possible.

Shortly after her conversation with the harbor master, Mickey went below and retrieved Darrel's pistol from the captain's berth. She carried it and the two boxes of ammunition to the cockpit.

Elena looked on as Mickey looked at the pistol a few moments and then tossed it, and the ammunition, into the ocean.

Mickey then glanced at Elena, who nodded slightly and then turned her head to peer at the approaching island.

They docked without incident and both Mickey and Elena spent several hours talking to a coast guard officer and an FBI agent. The incident with the two men on the open ocean did not come up in their conversations.

The coast guard officer said they were notified by a Janet Summers of Mickey's failure to check in after weeks passed with no contact. The coast guard notified officials in American Samoa and directed a search along the usual route from Hawaii to Samoa, but without some idea as to where the boat might be, there wasn't much more that could be done.

Mickey promised to call Janet as soon as possible.

The harbor master was kind enough to arrange lodging, which Mickey promised to pay for once she contacted her bank and had some money transferred.

Three days after arriving in Honolulu, Mickey boarded a flight to the States and settled into her seat for the long flight back.

CHAPTER 24

Mickey gazed out the backseat side window as the Uber driver wheeled the car through a modest Orlando community. She sat comfortably dressed in tight jeans, a fashionable top, and sandals. Her hair freshly styled. A small purse and a wood box sat on the seat beside her. She seemed not to notice the passing scenes as she thought about all she had been through over the past weeks, and why she came to be in Orlando on this day. She thought about the extra days she was in Hawaii, waiting for a duplicate New York license to be sent, and how she spent some of that time clothes shopping for her and Elena. She also made sure Elena saw a doctor. The exam apparently went well; Elena seemed pleased when she walked out of the exam room. Money hadn't been a problem. She remembered her bank codes and was able to transfer money to a local bank once she had access to a computer. The bank president accommodated her lack of identification once she explained the situation. And she thought about Elena at the airport for her flight to Tahiti and her transformation from a totally nude, scared, little girl, to the much more confident, fully clothed young woman that boarded the plane. Mickey intended to keep the promise she made to visit Elena's island home. Mickey also thought about the report she read in the Honolulu-Star newspaper about the escape from jail of two men caught in the act of raping a young girl in Hilo. Their description matched the two men Mickey encountered on her way to Hawaii. The search for the two men had been expanded to all the islands, but up to that point had failed to locate their whereabouts. Mickey wondered how long authorities would search before they gave up the hunt.

The car pulling to the curb in front of a single-story house brought Mickey out of her reverie. She fished in her purse and then handed the driver a few bills as a tip. She believed in tipping the driver, even though the ride had been paid through the app on her new cell phone.

The driver nodded and smiled. "I'll be cruising the area; there's a good chance you'll get me for the return trip."

"Thank you," Mickey said, as she opened the door and stepped to the sidewalk with her purse and the wood box. She closed the door and watched as the car pulled away. She then turned to face the concrete block house with the manicured lawn and shrubs.

She walked to the front door, pushed the doorbell, and heard a chime from inside. A few seconds later she heard the doorknob jiggle and then the door swung open.

An attractive young woman, maybe a little older than Mickey, filled the opening. She wore shorts and a t-shirt. No shoes. "I'm not interested in buying anything today," she said, as she smiled and then started to close the door.

"Clara Stevens?" Mickey asked.

The woman paused and then opened the door wider as she stepped closer. "Yes. Do I know you?"

"My name is Mick… Michelle Stewart. I was with your father when he died."

Clara stared at Mickey for several seconds. "You knew my father."

"Yes, briefly. He saved my life, actually."

Clara opened the door still wider and motioned for Mickey to step inside.

Mickey stepped into a small foyer and glanced at the great room immediately off to the side. The house appeared to be nicely furnished.

"What can I do for you?" Clara asked, as she closed the door. She motioned Mickey into the great room and then to take a seat on a sofa.

Mickey sat and placed her purse and the wood box next to her. "I thought you might like to know how he died."

"Can I get you something to drink?" Clara asked.

Mickey smiled. "Some water?"

Clara nodded and then stepped into a kitchen at the far side of the great room.

Mickey perused the room, paying particular attention to the photos. There were several on the walls and on the tables. They depicted Clara, a man about Clara's age, and two young children. There were no pictures of Clara's father.

Clara returned to the room and set a glass of ice water on the glass table in front of Mickey. "I haven't seen my dad in many years."

Mickey took a sip of the water and then replaced the glass. "I met him on Palmyra Island, in the middle of the Pacific, a few weeks ago. That's where I washed up, following the loss of the boat I was on and the death of my sister and brother-in-law."

Clara raised an eyebrow and then took a seat in a chair facing Mickey.

"Maybe I should start at the beginning."

Clara nodded and then reclined back in the chair.

Mickey explained the loss of the boat, Susan, and Thomas, and how she floated in the Pacific for days. She described first seeing Travis and how he helped her recover. She then explained why Travis came to be on the island and why he had no intention of leaving.

"So he died of cancer there on the island?"

"No. He died of a knife to the chest while saving my life, once again."

Clara shifted in the chair and waited for Mickey to continue.

Mickey described the encounter with Darrel and Raphael, her intent to go with them on their cruiser, and how they turned out to be human traffickers. She told Clara about the altercation on the beach, the death of the two men, and Travis's demise. She then described finding Elena and how they used Travis's boat to return to Hawaii.

Clara stared off into the room for several seconds before returning her gaze to Mickey. "I appreciate you coming all the way here to let me know. Like I said, I have not seen or heard from him in years. In a way, I guess, he was already dead. We weren't that close."

Mickey glanced at the wood box.

Clara followed her gaze. "Is that something for me?"

"It is," Mickey said. "During our days on the island he talked about you, about how he left when you were only ten, how he regretted leaving you like that, and how he hoped his leaving would not continue to shadow your life. In a way, his story helped me understand my own situation with my father, who left when I was ten. The difference is, my father didn't leave anything behind." Mickey placed her hand on the box. "I found the box on your dad's boat after he died. It contains photos and letters, letters he wrote to you, but never mailed."

"You read the letters?"

"Some of them. It's evident that he loved you and regretted to some degree what he did. I thought you should have what's in the box." Mickey placed the box on the table and then pushed the box slightly toward Clara.

"I appreciate the trouble you've gone through, but like I said, it's been a long time. I've built a life without him."

Mickey smiled. "It wasn't your fault that your father left. It wasn't my fault that my father left. Coming here was something I needed to do, as much for myself as for you."

Clara nodded. "I have almost no photographs of him," Clara said.

"Now you do," Mickey said, as she patted the box.

Clara dropped her chin, peered at the box, and nodded.

"I do have one favor to ask," Mickey said.

Clara raised her chin. "Yes?"

"I wonder if you would allow me to bring your father back here for burial."

"As far as I'm concerned—," Clara stopped and peered into Mickey's eyes for several seconds. She then let out a deep exhale. "I think I would like that."

"Perhaps we can do it together," Mickey said, as she stood.

Clara stood and extended her hand. "I think I would like that as well." Clara ushered Mickey to the door. "Thank you for coming."

Mickey shook her hand and smiled. Mickey stepped through the open door, but then stopped and turned back to Clara. "By the way, your father's boat, your boat now, is in the Honolulu yacht harbor. It's probably worth a lot. The harbormaster has the back story, and will help you deal with the boat."

"Thank you," Clara said.

They exchanged phone numbers and then Mickey stepped off toward the curb. She glanced back and smiled at Clara, still standing in the doorway.

Clara raised her hand in a slight wave.

***

Mickey, dressed in professional business attire, pushed through the glass door to Jackson Advertising. The receptionist was absent and the desk empty, so Mickey pressed a security code into the keypad, pushed the door open, and proceeded into the main work area. As she stepped into the corridor and proceeded past the various people at their desks, they all stopped what they were doing and stared at Mickey. She smiled at everyone as she passed without saying anything. Just short of reaching Janet's desk, the room erupted.

Everyone pressed forward and surrounded Mickey.

With her way blocked, she greeted everyone, returned their hugs, and acknowledged their affection.

One middle-aged female in particular lingered with her hand wrapped around Mickey's arm. "We weren't sure we'd ever see you again."

"There were times when I wondered the same thing," Mickey said. She thanked everyone and then excused herself as she proceeded down the corridor. She caught Janet coming out of Mickey's office.

Janet froze with her mouth open when she saw Mickey. Janet rushed forward and grabbed Mickey in a bear hug. "I was so worried when you didn't call from Samoa and greatly relieved when you called from Hawaii."

"I know," Mickey said. She then stepped back and grabbed Janet by the shoulders. "Janet, I'll be leaving the firm."

Janet cocked her head. "What do you mean?"

"I've given it a lot of thought. I'll be starting my own firm. And you're welcome to join me."

Janet froze, clearly troubled. She stared into Mickey's eyes as she took a step back and let her arms flop to her side. "What about Jack," she finally said.

At that moment, Jack rushed from his office and hurried down the corridor toward Mickey and Janet. His usually manicured hair mussed slightly.

Mickey, unmoved, watched as he approached. She thought his face expressed actual excitement over Mickey's return.

"Mickey, we were so worried—," he corrected himself. "I was worried," he said more seriously. "But now you're back." He gave her a hug and then stepped back, still holding her shoulders. "You look fantastic."

Mickey stepped back from his grasp and peered into his eyes for a moment. She then steadied her stance. "First, my name is Michelle. Second, you and I are finished. And third, I quit."

Jack's eyebrows narrowed, and he stared into Mickey's eyes for a long moment with his mouth gaped open. Finally he shook his head. "What do you mean?"

Mickey tightened her lips with the corners turned up slightly. She subtly shook her head and then turned to her office. She walked off as Jack and Janet stood staring. She returned a few seconds later with her briefcase in one hand and a picture of Susan and Thomas in the other. She stopped in front of Janet, raised one eyebrow, and then proceeded down the corridor without looking at Jack or saying another word.

Janet grabbed her sweater from her chair and her purse and then fell in behind Mickey. She looked back at Jack. "I guess I quit, too."

Mickey and Janet continued down the corridor, past the cubicles with everyone staring, and through the wood door.

They stepped from the elevator and exited the building to the sidewalk. Mickey followed Janet's gaze up the side of the building to the top floor.

"Do you know what you're doing?" Janet asked, as she returned her gaze to Mickey.

"I do," Mickey said. She nodded her head and then looked down the street. "I really do."

A REQUEST FROM THE AUTHOR

Thank you for reading *Surrounded By The Blue*. I hope you enjoyed the story as much as I enjoyed writing it. I do have one request. I ask that you please take a few moments to enter a product review on your Amazon 'Orders' page. Independent authors depend on reviews to get their books noticed. And reviews also help make my future books better. A few moments of your time would be much appreciated. I look forward to reading your thoughts. — **Victor Zugg**

ABOUT THE AUTHOR

Victor Zugg is a former US Air Force officer and OSI special agent who served and lived all over the world. Given his extensive travels and opportunities to settle anywhere, it is ironic that he now resides in Florida, only a few miles from his hometown of Orlando. He credits the warm temperatures for that decision.

Check out the author's other novels—*Solar Plexus (1), Near Total Eclipse (Solar Plexus 2)*, and *From Near Extinction*.

Made in the USA
Columbia, SC
22 August 2020

17368533R00183